# PRAISE FOR

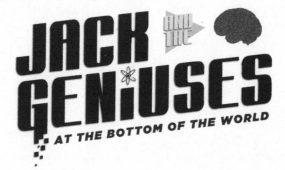

### AT THE BOTTOM OF THE WORLD

"The scientists are diverse, the educational and entertainment values are high, and there's even good end matter . . . making this a promising series start."
—*Bulletin of the Center for Children's Books*

"This fast-paced, science-themed mystery is a strong first outing, sure to leave readers awaiting this team's next adventure."
—*Publishers Weekly*

"This is a fantastic start to a new series that includes STEM concepts, facts, and excitement about the scientific world."
—*School Library Connection*

"Fast-paced enough to engage even reluctant readers, informative without being didactic, and entertaining: a solid series start."
—*Kirkus*

# BILL NYE
## & GREGORY MONE

### ILLUSTRATED BY
### NICK ILUZADA

AMULET BOOKS • NEW YORK

THE LIBRARY OF CONGRESS HAS CATALOGED THE HARDCOVER EDITION AS FOLLOWS:

NAMES: NYE, BILL, AUTHOR. 1 MONE, GREGORY, AUTHOR.
1 ILUZADA, NICHOLAS, ILLUSTRATOR.
TITLE: AT THE BOTTOM OF THE WORLD / BY BILL NYE AND GREGORY MONE ; ILLUSTRATED BY NICHOLAS ILUZADA.
DESCRIPTION: NEW YORK : AMULET BOOKS, 2017. 1 SERIES: JACK AND THE GENIUSES ; I 1 SUMMARY: TRAVELING TO ANTARCTICA FOR A PRESTIGIOUS SCIENCE COMPETITION, TWELVE-YEAR-OLD JACK AND HIS GENIUS FOSTER SIBLINGS, AVA AND MATT, BECOME CAUGHT UP IN A MYSTERY INVOLVING A MISSING SCIENTIST.
IDENTIFIERS: LCCN 2016047915 1 ISBN 9781419723032 (HARDBACK)
SUBJECTS: 1 CYAC: SCIENCE—FICTION. 1 SCIENTISTS—FICTION.
1 GENIUS—FICTION. 1 ORPHANS—FICTION. 1 BROTHERS AND SISTERS—FICTION. 1 ADVENTURE AND ADVENTURERS—FICTION. 1 ANTARCTICA—FICTION.
1 BISAC: JUVENILE FICTION / SCIENCE & TECHNOLOGY. 1 JUVENILE FICTION / SCIENCE FICTION. 1 JUVENILE FICTION / ACTION & ADVENTURE / GENERAL.
CLASSIFICATION: LCC PZ7.1.N94 AT 2017 1 DDC [FIC]—DC23
LC RECORD AVAILABLE AT HTTPS://LCCN.LOC.GOV/2016047915

PAPERBACK ISBN 978-1-4197-3288-1

ORIGINALLY PUBLISHED IN HARDCOVER BY AMULET BOOKS IN 2017
TEXT COPYRIGHT © 2017 BILL NYE
JACKET AND INTERIOR ILLUSTRATIONS COPYRIGHT © 2017 NICK ILUZADA

PRINTED AND BOUND IN U.S.A.
10 9 8 7 6 5 4 3 2 1

AMULET BOOKS ARE AVAILABLE AT SPECIAL DISCOUNTS WHEN PURCHASED IN QUANTITY FOR PREMIUMS AND PROMOTIONS AS WELL AS FUNDRAISING OR EDUCATIONAL USE. SPECIAL EDITIONS CAN ALSO BE CREATED TO SPECIFICATION. FOR DETAILS, CONTACT SPECIALSALES@ABRAMSBOOKS.COM OR THE ADDRESS BELOW.

**ABRAMS** The Art of Books
195 Broadway, New York, NY 10007
abramsbooks.com

FOR EVERY KID OF
ANY AGE WHO
SEEKS KNOWLEDGE
AND ADVENTURE
—B.N.

TO CLARE
—G.M.

# CONTENTS

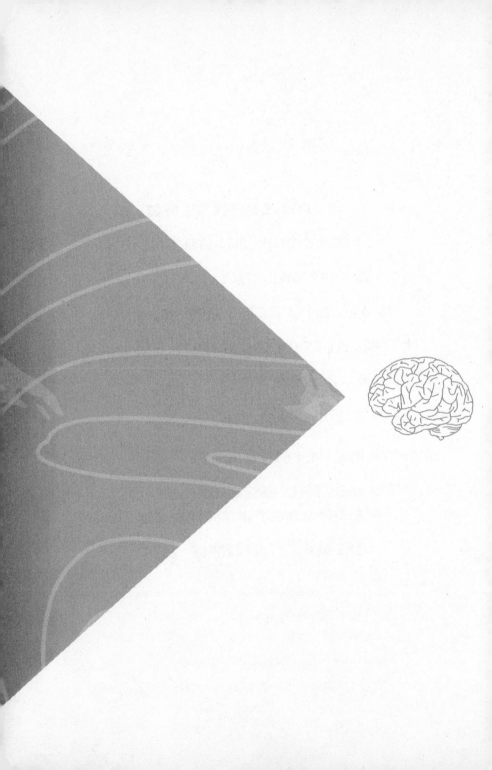

# I

# ATTACK OF THE PIZZABOT

**I**N THE ALLEY, FRED HOVERED ABOVE US, AWAITING instructions. His four spinning blades buzzed like dragonflies. Ava tapped the cracked screen of her old smartphone, then dragged her finger slowly from the bottom to the top. Fred rose higher. "Should I start?" Ava asked.

"Absolutely," I said.

Matt leaned forward and looked over at me, his head tilted slightly. "You're sure this is legal, Jack?"

Nope. Definitely not. I'd already checked, and this sort of thing was completely against the law. But the neighborhood wasn't even awake yet. There was no one around to catch us, and we absolutely had to find out what was going on in the building across the street. "It's totally fine," I lied. "Trust me."

Fred spun, tilted forward, and zoomed toward his target. Did I mention that he was a robot? A plastic cube, basically,

1

along with a camera, some electronic brains, motors and batteries, and miniature fans attached to four mechanical arms. A pretty simple drone, I guess, until you figure that my twelve-year-old sister built him from scratch. At our kitchen table. From a collection of spare parts.

The name was Ava's choice, and although Matt guessed the initials stood for Flying Robotic Electronic Drone, she swore she just liked the name Fred. By that point she'd also built a dangerously fast motorized skateboard called Pedro and a talking toaster named Bob. Pedro had sent me tumbling into a pile of overstuffed trash bags a few weeks earlier, and poor Bob exploded after some sesame seeds caught fire. That was a real shame. I liked Bob. He had a nice, light touch with bagels.

As Fred flew higher, my brother and sister huddled around the screen of her laptop, but I crept out of the alley and watched the robot approach the strange building. We live in Williamsburg, Brooklyn, across the East River from New York City, and new apartments and offices are always popping up around us. Most of them are pretty similar, but then this one went up last year that was just plain weird. Ten stories tall and skinny, the outside a chessboard of reflective-glass windows, the top floor covered with a ring of solar panels that resemble some kind of high-tech head-band. The structure has no front door. Or back door. Or side door. No entrance or exit at all. None of the windows ever open, and because they reflect light like mirrors, you cannot see inside. A balcony was tucked into the north side of the building on the third floor, but did we ever spot anyone up there? An old lady in her flowery bathrobe drinking coffee? A bald man in a ribbed tank top scratching his hairy armpits as he stretched? A kid braiding the fur of her pet llama? Nope. Not once.

So we'd started guessing what really went on inside. Hypothesizing, as Matt would say. I was hoping the new tower was the headquarters of an evil billionaire plotting world domination. Ava suggested it might be an interna-tionally renowned superspy's secret office. But Matt's bet was typically logical. He said some company probably kept its computers there.

After we'd been watching the building for months with-out discovering a single clue, I begged Ava to use Fred. I bribed her. I pleaded. Once I even pretended to cry. Eventu-ally she agreed, and now our mechanical spy was rising up toward that third-floor balcony. I rushed back into the alley. The screen of Ava's laptop showed the view from the robot's camera, so we could watch the scene from Fred's perspective.

Ava used her smartphone to steer him forward for a closer look at the balcony. I held my breath.

And I sighed.

No spy telescope. No jet-pack landing pad. No laser gun mounted on a swiveling turret. And certainly no llama.

"Told you," Matt said. "It's a data center."

Ava leaned my way and started to explain. "That's where companies house the servers they—"

"I know." To be honest, I didn't know, but it's super annoying to have your genius brother and sister teaching you stuff all the time.

Something flashed across Ava's screen. "Wait, what was that?" she asked.

I ran back out onto the sidewalk and stared across the street. Fred was gone. A glass door to the balcony was open for the very first time, but no one was in sight, and I couldn't see inside, either. Had Fred fallen? There was no sign of him on the pavement below the building. I held my breath and listened, but I couldn't hear the buzz of his fans.

Returning to the alley, I peered over my sister's shoulder just as the robot's camera view went dark. The signal on the laptop blinked out. "Fred!" Ava cried.

"What just happened?" I asked.

"I don't know," she said. "I think someone inside grabbed him."

My heart started pounding. Ava had spent months constructing that robot. She'd worked so hard and grown so frustrated that I'd actually caught her eyes tearing up once or twice. And my sister never cried. Still, she'd stuck with it, and once Fred flew, she was as happy as I'd ever seen her. Now the drone was gone, and it was all my fault.

Ava slammed her laptop shut with unusual force, shoved it into her shoulder bag, and stomped out of the alley. One side of her mouth peaked into an angry snarl.

"Wait!" I said. "Where are you going?"

"To get Fred."

I followed her across the pothole-lined street. "What are you going to do?"

She locked her fingers and cracked her knuckles. "Shout, yell, make some noise until someone answers."

"You'll wake the whole neighborhood."

"Too bad. I'm getting Fred back."

As we squeezed between two parked cars with dented bumpers, I stared up at the balcony. "Let me try something first."

"It's not like there's a front door," Matt called out from a few steps behind us. "You can't just knock, you know."

No, but I could climb. Most of my experience was with trees, as I'd spent pretty much all of third and fourth grade hiding from my foster family in a backyard oak. Normally

I only scaled buildings when we locked ourselves out of our apartment, but this was an exception. I hurried ahead of Ava and inspected the building's walls up close. The edges of the square windows were deep enough to grip. The building sloped in slightly as it rose, so I wouldn't be going straight up. I was sure I could make it. And if someone yelled at me? I was just a kid trying to get his toy robot back.

Matt leaned back against the building, clasped his hands, and held them at his waist. I tightened my shoelaces, grabbed his shoulders, planted my right foot in his hands, and pushed myself up. At fifteen, my older brother was already taller than most adults, so he was a good ladder, and the climbing was easier than expected. The window edges were a few inches deep. The big problem was the windows themselves. You couldn't see through them from the outside, but they were also strangely slippery, as if they were coated with some kind of invisible grease.

"What's wrong?" Ava asked.

I told her. Matt ran one finger across the glass, then waved it below his nose and dabbed it against his tongue. "Interesting," he said. "No smell. Not much of a taste, either." He walked a few feet and swiped another pane. "All the windows seem to be coated with it."

"I wonder why," Ava said.

"Maybe it's to prevent people from climbing," he said.

7

"Thanks," I said. "That's really encouraging."

Moving slowly, I focused on my grip. Between the first and second floors I stopped to rest.

"How much farther?" I asked.

"Three meters," Matt said.

"Or about the height of a basketball hoop," Ava translated. "Be careful, Jack. Take your time."

"But hurry up," Matt said.

A car turned the corner and started rolling toward us.

"Act natural!" Ava said.

She faked a laugh. Matt copied her. My task was a little more difficult. How are you supposed to act natural when you're clinging to the side of a glass building at six in the morning?

The car cruised past without slowing, but the neighborhood was definitely coming to life. Delivery trucks were rumbling down the avenue a block away. A small bell chimed as the owner of the German deli across the street propped open his door. I needed to hustle.

An arm's length from the balcony, I reached for the next window edge, and the fingers of my right hand slipped. I tried to push them against the glass, hoping to stop myself from swinging. But my right hand slid like a hockey puck across a frozen pond. The fingers of my left hand lost their hold. My feet lost contact with the building. And a second later I was airborne, falling backward—a bird without wings.

My landing pad was going to be a wide square of concrete. I wrapped my head in my bare arms and shut my eyes hard.

Matt shouted.

Ava yelled.

But the sound of their cries was muffled by an explosive hiss.

I braced for a brutal slam against the pavement, then hit . . . something else. Instead of smashing down onto the concrete, I bounced. In midair again, I opened my eyes and glanced down. The hiss had been the sound of some kind of cushion inflating, and now I was gently bouncing to a stop on what looked like a bouncy house from a kindergartener's birthday party. The material was smooth to the touch and almost shiny. I rolled off the cushion.

My siblings' eyes were as big as golf balls.

"Did that really just happen?" Ava asked.

"I would've caught you," Matt said.

No way he could have caught me.

The three of us leaped back as the lifesaving surface collapsed. Within seconds it was completely deflated. Then the building started to slurp it up like a strand of spaghetti, sucking it back inside through a slit near the sidewalk, just

9

below the first row of windows. Ava pointed, speechless. The gap was smaller than a mail slot. Once the cushion was completely coiled back into the building, Matt crouched forward to peer through the tiny opening. But before he had the chance to see inside, a steel panel slid shut. Whatever had saved me from broken bones or worse was gone as quickly as it had appeared.

Matt pulled at his hair with both hands. "I don't like this," he said.

"Why not? That was awesome," I said.

"Someone must be watching us." Matt turned, scanning the block, then scowled in the direction of the alley across the street. "That camera over there, on the fire escape. Was that there before?"

He pointed at a black device about the size of an energy-drink can, with a lens at the top. Who cared about some security camera? I'd just been saved by a magical cushion after falling thirty feet off the side of a building!

"I would've noticed," Ava said.

The camera suddenly unfurled two long black wings, sprang off the fire escape, glided downward, then flapped like a mechanical hawk, narrowly dodging the roof of a rusted van parked at the corner. The flying camera soared higher as it crossed the road, swooped over our heads, then dipped again and dropped straight onto the balcony of our mystery building.

"Whoa."

"Let's get out of here," Matt said. He grabbed the back of my shirt.

"You two can go," Ava said. "But I'm getting Fred back."

She walked along the side of the building, leaning in close to look for another opening. At a few points she knocked. She pushed against one of the windows as if it might pop open. Matt kept turning and glancing over his shoulder. Maybe he was worried that a fleet of black cars was going to roar up, screech to a stop at the curb, and spit out a dozen secret agents in dark glasses. Or maybe that was just me.

"We already looked for a door," I reminded Ava.

"Maybe we missed something." She raised her eyebrows at Matt. "Are you going to help or just stand there looking scared?"

"Fine," Matt barked back.

As my brother crossed the road for a different view of the building, I wondered if there was an easier solution. What if we just had to ask nicely? I pulled out my pocket-size spiral notebook, dashed out a quick but sincere apology to the owner of the building, and tore the page loose. At the curb I found a chunk of asphalt about the size of a large green grape, wrapped the paper around it, aimed, and tossed my message up toward the balcony. Once the little rock left my hand, I wondered whether I should've stopped to think through my plan. An apology delivered by broken window probably wouldn't be that effective. I closed my eyes and winced, waiting for the sound of shattering glass. Thankfully, my message landed safely.

On the street. But on my third attempt I succeeded. Without breaking a single pane.

Ava returned to the front of the building. "What did you just do?" she asked.

"Nothing," I lied.

"Hey," Matt said, crossing back over to our side of the street. "Follow me. I think I know the way in."

"What? How?" Ava asked.

We waited as a blue minivan clunked down the street. Then Matt explained as he led us back across the street to the alley. "I was thinking about rabbits."

"Rabbits?" I asked.

"Yes, and their warrens in particular. For safety reasons they have multiple entrances and exits to their homes, and none are right next to the main living area."

"You think rabbits live in there?" I asked. The words were hardly out of my mouth before I started wishing I could reel them back in unsaid.

"No, Jack," Matt said. "I don't think that building is occupied by giant hyper intelligent bunnies."

I tried to stop myself from imagining those rabbits. I was unsuccessful. Would they still eat carrots? Would they order takeout from the burrito place up the block? Would they wear tuxedos? Yes. They would absolutely prefer elegant evening attire.

Naturally Ava understood what Matt was trying to say. "So the front door is here across the street?" she asked. "But where?"

"Well, rabbits cover their entrances with leaves and brush—the sort of thing you'd normally find around a field or lawn or hill."

Now I was really lost.

"The Dumpster?" Ava guessed, pointing.

"Exactly," Matt said. "It's the sort of thing you'd expect to find in an alley." He hurried over and tapped the side with his fingers. "Look. The paint has barely been scratched. I bet it's not even a Dumpster at all. What if it's some kind of elevator?"

I opened the container's heavy black lid. A hurricane of horrible smells attacked my nostrils. The stench was like a combination of rotting ham sandwiches and spoiled milk. "Nope, it's definitely a Dumpster."

My brother's shoulders sank. "Really?"

"Wait." Ava was crouching at the base. "This thing is on

rails, and there's some kind of electric motor under here. But I can't figure out how to activate it."

Ava swept her fingers along the underside of the Dumpster. Matt checked near the lid, then ran his hands across the logo painted on the left side.

"What does H-W-I stand for?" I asked.

"I don't know," Matt said, "but look closely at the i."

The dot above the lowercase letter was actually a small square piece of see-through plastic, with a red button behind it. Matt and Ava both stood frozen, unwilling or unable to take the next step. See, that's one of my roles. When you hang out with geniuses, it's hard to find a way to be useful. So I plan. I scheme. Occasionally I talk my siblings into situations they'd avoid on their own. But that never feels like enough, so I'm usually the one who takes the risks. Sometimes that means testing a rocket-powered skateboard named Pedro. Sometimes it means jabbing at a cleverly hidden button to see what happens next.

I used a fingernail to pry open the plastic cover, pushed the red button with my thumb, then jumped back as the Dumpster instantly slid to my left along the alley wall, revealing a large rectangular hole in the pavement and a set of aluminum stairs. While Matt and I stared in shock, Ava started right down. "I'm coming to get you, Fred," she called.

"Wait—" Matt said.

There was no point trying to stop Ava. Her boots clanged on the metal stairs as she descended. Matt followed. Three steps down he tripped and had to grab the railing to prevent himself from tumbling to the bottom. Poor Matt. His feet had stretched two sizes since the winter, and he was still figuring out how to steer them around. Normally I laughed when he stumbled, so he glared up at me immediately. I held up my hands. "I didn't say anything!"

The air inside was cool but not cold; it smelled slightly of bleach. Dull yellow lights shined below us. Halfway down the stairs, I nearly leaped when the Dumpster above slid back over the opening in the pavement. Ava didn't react, though, so I certainly wasn't going to admit to being petrified.

The stairs stopped at the top of an enormous escalator rolling down into total darkness. We paused. I tried to look tough but cool, like one of those old-fashioned fighter pilots in their leather jackets and dark sunglasses.

"Jack, do you need to go to the bathroom?" Matt asked.

Apparently my "tough" face wasn't working.

"We're not going down there, are we?" Matt asked Ava.

"You can wait here if you want," Ava said.

After matching deep breaths, my brother and I followed her. Lights began brightening in front of us, dimming at our backs. Ava was smiling when she turned around.

"Smart lighting. Sensors activate the bulbs when you get close."

The escalator ended two or three stories down, but another was right beside it. The air had a dusty and metallic smell now, and Matt guessed we were a hundred feet below the pavement when we finally reached the bottom—a square platform I could cross in three steps. The air was colder here; I shivered. In front of us was a normal-looking door. Neither of my siblings moved. I raised an eyebrow and looked at each of them. They shrugged.

My turn again.

I pushed through the door. It closed behind us. The carpeted room was shaped like a hexagon. Three sides had wide, deep, and very comfortable-looking blue couches. One of the other walls had a door with a long desk posted in front. To our left was a powerful-looking steel door with a painting of a dog hanging beside it. A schnauzer, I think.

I walked toward that door. The carpet was soft. It smelled new.

"No company name or anything, huh?" Ava noted.

"Maybe it really is a spy's headquarters, Ava," I said.

I scanned a pile of packages, letters, and thick catalogs on the floor below the dog portrait. Each was addressed to one of several different "H.W.I." companies. The only label with a person's name on it was a return address stuck to a yellowing envelope that looked like it had gotten into a street fight with a dozen other letters. The envelope was wrinkled, torn in places, and dotted with dried mud. The sender's name was Anna Donatelli, and her return address was Antarctica. "Check this out," I said. "A letter from the North Pole."

Matt walked over. "Antarctica is the South Pole," he said.

Sometimes I wished they'd just let me be wrong.

Matt pressed his head against the wall, inspecting the dog painting from the side. Then he held his hand below it. Smiling, he lifted the picture frame from the bottom. It swung open, revealing a metal chute.

"Cool way to get your mail," Ava remarked.

The door behind the desk opened with a low hiss. I resisted the urge to hide behind one of my siblings.

We waited. Nothing happened.

"Hello?" Matt called out. "We're sorry to bother you, but we're trying to find my sister's . . ."

His words trailed off as a tall red robot wheeled into the room. After living with Ava for almost two years, I knew it was a humanoid—a machine with two arms, a head, and two eyelike cameras. But she'd never shown me any videos of one like this before.

Matt apologized again, speaking slowly and clearly so the robot could understand him.

In a flat, emotionless voice the machine asked, "What are you doing here? This is private property."

Ava was smiling. "You can chat? That's amazing. We're sorry to intrude, but I lost my—"

"What are you doing here? This is private property. What are you doing here? This is private property." The robot began repeating itself, speaking faster each time.

"Something's wrong with its code," Ava said.

"Or it's angry," I suggested, backing toward the door to the stairs. I tried to turn the handle. "Uh, guys, the door's locked."

The robot moved out from behind the desk, rolling toward us on three large wheels, repeating its words faster and faster. A red light on its chest began flashing.

"Ava, what does that mean?" Matt asked.

"How should I know?"

"I think it means we need to find another way out," I said.

Matt sidestepped over to the steel door and pressed a circular button beside its frame.

The robot's light flashed brighter. Now its words were jammed together into a single crazed stream. "Whatareyou-doingherethis . . ."

With a slow creak, the steel door slid open, revealing an old-fashioned elevator car. Matt grabbed me and practically tossed me inside, then pulled Ava by the back of her shirt. "Get in! Get in!"

The humanoid opened a compartment in its chest.

The elevator door was closing at the pace of a garden-slug race. The robot pulled something out and flung it at us. I ducked the shot, and a yellowish clump splattered on the dark-wood paneling behind me. The elevator door was barely halfway closed. The robot was rolling closer. The machine threw something, striking Matt in the chest. My brother shouted and fell to the floor.

Ava kicked the door with the heel of her boot. Finally it slammed shut. The elevator lurched, and we felt ourselves riding up. Matt grabbed a clump of yellowish stuff from his shirt and hurled it against the wood paneling. It fell to the floor with a splat.

"Are you okay?" I asked.

He scooted away, pressing himself against the wall. Ava looked more bewildered than frightened. A big chunk of the stuff was hanging from the paneling behind me, too, and I reached out to touch it.

"Jack, no!" Matt said. "It could be toxic."

I leaned in closer and sniffed. The scent was familiar. I peeled the stuff from the wall, bit off a chunk, chewed, then spat it out. In our little family, I'm the closest thing to a cook, and this particular substance was the basis

19

of one of my signature meals. "It's just pizza dough," I said.

"So was that some kind of pizzabot?" Matt asked.

The elevator clanked to a stop before Ava could reply. The door rolled open and we stepped into a storeroom of some kind. The walls were lined with shelves. We were surrounded by jars of pickles and mayonnaise, plastic tubs of sauerkraut, and loaves of white bread. Matt slapped me on the shoulder with the back of his hand. He breathed out, long and hard, then smiled. "See? Multiple ways in and out, like rabbits."

There was a swinging wooden door on the other side of the storeroom. Ava nudged it open, and we stepped into the back of a deli that stank of burned coffee. Behind the counter, the German deli owner, with his long moustache and mustard-stained apron, started shouting at us, waving a long loaf of unsliced bread. So we ran. Out through the deli's front door, past the alley, around the corner. Despite his athletic frame, my brother is challenged as a runner. Normally he'd eat it at least twice on a sprint that long. For once, though, I was glad Matt didn't trip and fall, and we put at least four blocks behind us before we stopped.

Between breaths Matt asked, "How . . . in the world . . . did all that just happen?"

I was still too startled to speak. The lifesaving cushion.

The flying security camera. The Dumpster entrance to a secret room. The attack by a pizza-dough-flinging robot. Honestly, I was still processing everything, and my heart was racing with a mix of excitement and fear. But my sister was somewhere else emotionally. The thrill of escape had faded. Now all that was left was disappointment. Her eyes were slightly closed. Her mouth formed a flat line. While Matt and I had just survived a strange and wild adventure— a morning like none other—Ava had lost a friend. I was responsible. And I had to find a way to get Fred back.

# 2

# AN UNUSUAL INVITATION

**AYBE THIS IS A GOOD TIME TO INTRODUCE**
myself. Yeah. Probably. I'm Jack. I've had four
sets of parents, none very good at the job. The
last pair couldn't even scramble an egg. Ava
and Matt are my sister and brother by law—not blood—but
you'd guess that at a glance. Matt has short dark hair, olive
skin, and a nose that takes a sharp downward turn at the
halfway point. His gray eyes bulge out like telescopes, and
over the last year he grew too fast to maintain what little
balance and coordination he once had. At fifteen he's always
stumbling, knocking over water glasses, and bumping into
doorways with his wide shoulders.

Ava and I are the same age, but she's a few inches taller,
with skin the color of coffee, a round face, and long eyelashes.
Her wavy brown hair is always yanked back in a ponytail,
and her wide eyes and bright smile can melt even the mean-
est adults. When she walks, the heels of her high-top boots

barely touch the ground, and her small hands are scarred in places—a hazard of building her mechanical marvels. Me? I'm as pale as a paper towel, with brown eyes, straight blond hair that Ava says I comb too often, and perfect teeth. Okay. That's not true. They're slightly crooked. Also, unlike Matt, I don't have any muscles yet, but I'm only twelve. I'm hoping they'll show up soon.

But enough about the looks. The important thing here is that my siblings are geniuses. You've probably heard of them, since they get most of the attention. Not many people know that their bestselling book of poems, *The Lonely Orphans*, was actually my idea. Sure, the verses are really sappy and "roses are red" simple, but we needed cash, Ava and Matt are clever with rhymes, and I knew the book would sell. Moms and grandmothers really eat up that heartbroken orphan stuff. Not into poetry? Well I'm sure you've seen that video of the kid giving CPR to a puppy. That was me. Fifteen million hits, thank you very much. The whole thing was fake—the little guy was just sleeping—but it worked a public relations miracle for us.

Also, we're not really orphans anymore. Call us independent. Or, as Ava likes to say, autonomous. A few years ago,

Ava, Matt, and I ended up with the same foster parents. The two of them were already winning awards for their brains, skipping from one grade to the next like stones across a pond, and one night I had an idea. We'd just made ourselves dinner, because Alice and Bob were out, as usual. Halfway through my bowl of boxed macaroni and cheese with sliced hot dogs, I glanced up at my brother and sister and asked, "Can't we just get rid of the adults and take care of ourselves?" At first Matt said it was illegal. I asked if he was sure. Then Ava repeated my question. Matt stared at the wall for a few minutes, then got up, walked out the door, and spent the next two days in the library of a local law school. Alice and Bob didn't even notice he was gone. Matt came back as if it had only been a few minutes since we'd asked him the question. "No," he said, "I'm not sure. We might have a chance."

In the end, it took several court cases, some powerful lawyers, a book of cheesy poems to make enough money to pay the lawyers, a fake puppy video to convince the public to love us, and a brilliantly acted, fake-tear-filled speech by Ava. But we got rid of Alice and Bob. I guess you could say we divorced our foster parents. And, aside from all the newspapers describing us as "two young geniuses and their brother," I was thrilled with how it all worked out. A nice lady from Social Services named Min checks on us weekly, but we're pretty much flying solo now. Matt takes college classes, and Ava and I both homeschool; we meet with our instructors online. My grades are fine, I guess, but I never feel all that smart. That's one of the downsides of living with geniuses.

So, anyway, we live on our own in a small Brooklyn apartment, and after getting chased out of the deli by the bread-waving German, that's where we waited for the next three days, desperately trying to come up with a plan to retrieve Ava's robot. Three separate times I attempted to sneak back into the strange building without telling my siblings, but the Dumpster was locked, and the guy in the deli tried to attack me with a squeeze bottle of mustard every time I got close to his front door.

Neither Ava nor Matt were all that happy with me, because they'd figured out I'd lied about our little spy operation being legal. Using a drone to peer into someone's windows is totally against the law, and one of the terms of our "autonomous" childhood was that we had to be on nearly perfect behavior at all times. So now there was a chance we'd lose more than a homemade robot. I was sure Min was going to show up at any moment and tell us we were going to be split up and thrown into different foster homes. I'd end up with a family of asparagus farmers in Canada. They'd be the kind of people who flushed the toilet only once a day to save water.

25

That's the way I thought it was going to work, anyway.

But for seventy-two hours there was no knock at our door.

Our phone didn't ring.

And I started to wonder if we were safe.

Then, a little after six o'clock on Sunday night, Matt called out from the kitchen. The room was really more of a workshop. Sure, it housed a microwave and a fridge, and my little coffeemaker was tucked away in a back corner of a counter. But Ava had replaced the oven with a 3-D printer and taken most of the cabinet and drawer space for her spare parts and tools. The kitchen table was crammed with computers and circuit boards.

My brother and sister were standing in front of her laptop. "What's up?" I asked.

"You just got an e-mail from Henry Witherspoon."

I shrugged. "Who's he?"

"A scientist, an inventor, a pretty amazing engineer. And the head of Henry Witherspoon Industries. The guy has worked on rockets, robots, electric cars, space telescopes—"

"He helped invent the nose vacuum, too."

Ava knew how to speak my language. I'd been dying to get a nose vacuum for months, but they were too expensive. Basically, instead of a tissue, you just placed this device, about the size of a Sharpie cap, up your nostril, and it

26

automatically sucked out any unwanted material. "Why is he writing to me?"

Matt spread his arms wide. "Because that was his building we tried to break into!"

"Oh."

Arms crossed, Ava stared at me. "And it appears that you may have written him a note?"

"Yes, well . . . is he mad?"

"No, that's the thing. He's inviting us to dinner tonight."

"Then I should get dressed," I answered.

An hour later we were back in the alley, standing at the Dumpster. We were already late, and that part was my fault. We didn't get invited to dinner very often, so I'd wanted a few extra minutes to figure out what to wear. Is that so crazy? My siblings had thought so, but I took my time anyway, and settled on a nice blue button-down shirt, a striped bowtie, a pair of jeans, and black Samba sneakers. The bowtie was new, and it took me seven tries to get the knot just right.

"This entrance is under repair," a voice said from behind us.

All three of us spun around. A tall, thin man was standing there. A leather bag was slung over his shoulder. His eyes were wrinkled at the corners. His graying hair and slight beard were buzzed to the same length, and he wore a T-shirt with two buttons at the collar and an equation scrawled across the middle. He pointed at each of us in turn. "Ava, Matt, John. Yes?"

"Yes," Ava answered. "You're Henry Witherspoon?"

"Indeed," he said with a laugh. "Where are my manners? Excuse me, please."

"You can call me Jack," I said, extending my hand. "He prefers Matthew, though." My brother grimaced. He hates his full name. "It's an honor to meet you, Mr. Witherspoon."

We shook hands, and his was so huge, it practically swallowed mine. "Call me Hank," he said. "I must compliment you on your tie, Jack. I was once fond of such professorial attire myself." Before I could respond, his eyes lit up. He held up one of his long fingers, reached into his bag, and carefully removed Ava's drone. "You built this?" he said to Ava, holding Fred out to her.

She bit her lower lip and reached for him. I held my breath. The man had been nice enough so far, but this was the point at which we'd learn whether "Hank" Witherspoon was going to be a friend or an enemy. Thankfully, he passed Fred right to her. I was pretty much floating with relief.

"Don't worry," he continued. "The HR-4 grabbed it with a net normally used in the practice of lepidoptery. That's the study of butterflies, but you probably knew that." He pointed to one of Fred's propellers. "Those are repurposed computer fans?"

"That's right," Ava said, her voice nearly a whisper. "I had to file down the blades a little."

"An ingenious use of discarded technology. Waste not; want not. And the code you wrote for the guidance software is beautiful, too. Pure geek poetry. Better than that book of poems, certainly." He turned to me. "Although I should say that your effort to revive that puppy was truly heartwarming."

Before I could reply, Ava asked, "What's the HR-4?"

"A prototype robotic assistant. I believe you already met. The HR-4 tried to offer you pizza."

"Attacked us is more like it," I said.

Matt stepped in front of me, pointing at the long string of letters and symbols on Henry Witherspoon's shirt. "That's the equation for Einstein's general theory."

"I should hope you'd be able to pick that out, Matthew. Not bad for a fifteen-year-old. Of course, I was finishing college at your age. But still. Not bad."

Matt's smile flickered at the mixed compliment. He squinted at the side of the Dumpster, then pointed to the logo. "H-W-I—does that stand for Henry Witherspoon Industries?"

"Right again."

Ava was checking Fred to make sure nothing was broken. Matt was beaming so brightly, you'd think he'd just gotten a

29

compliment from Albert Einstein himself. Someone needed to think clearly here. "So, Mr. Wither—Hank," I said. "Do you want to tell us what's going on? You caught us spying on you. You got my note. Why did you invite us to dinner?"

He smiled. "We can discuss all that when we get inside."

We followed Hank out of the alley and into the deli. Through the shop's large glass display case I could see our German friend holding his hand over the mustard bottle like a cowboy preparing to draw his gun. When he spotted Hank, though, he gestured us toward his back room.

*"Entschuldigung,"* Ava said with a smile.

The man raised his large eyebrows and ever so slightly bowed in her direction.

"You speak German?" Hank asked.

"I'm learning," Ava said.

And she was probably going to be fluent within a week. Was there a German word for *show-off*?

"Does he work for you?" Matt asked.

"Franz? No. I own the building, and he's kind enough to let me use his storeroom."

Inside the back room Hank moved a roll of paper towels out of the way and pressed a few buttons on a keypad. After we rode the elevator down in silence, Hank hurried out, pushed through the door behind the desk, and waved toward the room beyond. "Welcome to my scientific playground!"

The inside of the building was a single open room, and it was like nothing I'd ever seen. We stood on a floor somewhere far below street level, and the ceiling loomed more than ten stories above us. Light streamed in through the upper windows. The air was humid and thick. High above us three or four birds were circling and screeching. Instead of separate floors, there were platforms attached to the walls. They were the size of large bedrooms, and they started all the way up near the ceiling and extended down in a spiral pattern. A giant would have been able to walk up them like the steps of a winding staircase. How normal humans moved from one to the other I couldn't figure out.

Hank crossed the space, giving us a rapid tour. The ground floor was about half the size of a football field. There was a twenty-foot-deep, crystal-clear, aboveground pool diagonally across from us in the far left corner. A small submarine floated at the surface. "That's the *Nautilus Redux*," Hank said, flicking his fingers toward the craft. "She's a little leaky." In another corner, a steep artificial hill covered with fake rocks and dirt rose up from the floor to a height of fifteen feet. Hank ignored that and pointed to an enclosed room with see-through walls and a layer of orange soil two feet deep. Inside, a robot with tracked wheels and solar panels was repeatedly bumping up against a small boulder. "That's my Mars simulation chamber," he said. "It's about as

close as you'll get to the surface of the Red Planet without climbing into a rocket ship."

A miniature racetrack looped around the lab benches, cabinets, and worktables in the center of the room. I stepped forward and pressed the toe of one sneaker down on the edge of the track; it felt like rubber.

"Made from recycled tires," Hank said. He kneeled at the edge and pushed his knuckles into the surface, then raised his eyebrows in the direction of a small car, half the size of a golf cart, cruising slowly toward us. "The track has sensors inside that pick up the slightest pressure. So it knows where the car is and how fast it's going."

Behind me, Matt said, "So it's a smart road?"

Hank sprang to his feet and patted my brother on the back. "Exactly!"

With his right hand down near his waist, Matt carried out the smallest fist-pump in history. I tried to think of something brilliant to add. I failed.

Ava was pointing skyward. "Are those drones?"

"Ah, yes, I thought you might like them. Ornithopters, technically. Drones that fly like birds, by flapping their wings."

Below the circling robots, a few of the tree-house-like platforms were home to tall, leafy plants and small trees.

Two were enclosed, the windows fogged and sweating. Greenhouses, I guessed. Three others were crowded with steel cylinders and tubes and various strange equipment.

Ava pointed to the miniature vehicle heading our way. "Is that self-driving?" she asked.

"Yes, it's basically a small version of a real car. The vehicle makes all the decisions. No need for a driver at all."

On the other side of the track there was a miniature junkyard, with a few old tires, a massive snowblower lying on its side, a pile of strange, shiny material, and some kind of giant catapult—the kind of contraption that launched boulders at castle walls. Except that a mannequin was seated where there should have been a rock.

Matt pointed to the shiny fabric. "That's what the cushion outside was made of, right?"

"Yes! I planned to have a cleaning crew wash the windows every week, so I installed that system in case one of them fell," Hank explained. "But once I made the windows self-cleaning, I didn't need the crew, so I never had the chance to test the system. I should thank you, Jack. And I suppose you should thank me, too, since that concrete would not have been a good landing site."

Matt jumped in before I had the chance. "The windows are self-cleaning? There was some kind of coating—"

"That's right! No dirt or grime will stick to them, and

all it takes is a little rain to rinse them clean. As for that cushion, the company that makes the material hired me to come up with some additional applications, and that rescue system was one of my first ideas."

"What else is the material used for?" Ava asked.

"The company's main goal is creating inflatable space habitats. And speaking of space . . ." Hank hurried over to a fat, cone-shaped structure about the size of a minivan. "What we have here is a prototype capsule for Mars astronauts. It's a scale model, obviously, and please don't tell anyone you saw it." He turned slowly, waving casually at an overwhelming mix of gadgets and devices and vehicles. "Look around, please. See that pair of metal legs over there? Firefighters could put those on and kick through the doors of burning buildings. Or you could strap into them and climb a mountain without getting tired." He pointed over his shoulder at the artificial hill in the corner. "I built that to test the robolegs, in fact."

This was all very interesting, and my siblings were drinking in Hank's every word, but in scanning the room I'd found something far more life-changing. The device that I believe to be the greatest invention of the twenty-first century was sitting on a workbench designated by a sign that read "Clutterbuck Prize." The nose vacuum was sleek, shiny, and beautifully simple, and it lay next to a dark, curly wig, a pair of boxer shorts, a metal cube the size and shape of a standard garbage can, and many other items.

I rushed over and picked up the vacuum.

"Go ahead, try it," Hank said.

My nose was only slightly stuffed at the time, but I lifted the little wonder to one nostril and waited with anticipation. The miniature motor inside whirred, and the force of the device was so powerful, it felt like aliens were trying to suck my brain out through a straw. I yanked the vacuum away from my nose. Immediately it shut off.

"It stings a little the first time, but how do you feel?"

I sniffed. A rush of humid air filled my nostrils. I smelled soil, metal, rubber. "Amazing," I admitted. Then I pointed to the table. "What's all this?"

"A few little ideas I've been developing, but most of these are former entries for the Clutterbuck Prize, an annual contest I judge," he said, pointing to the sign.

"What do these do?" I asked, grabbing the pair of boxer shorts.

"Self-drying underwear. At the touch of a button you can release a supply of pressurized air in the waistband that dries the fabric instantly."

Hank spun around as his malfunctioning robot friend rolled into the room. "Oh, good! The HR-4 is here to take your orders. Matthew? Ava? You'll have pizza, I hope?"

"What's that?" Matt asked, pointing to a large and very comfortable-looking stuffed leather chair.

The chair itself appeared normal enough.

But it was moving.

Quickly.

Hank grabbed a laptop from a countertop and pecked at the keys with his index finger. But the chair accelerated straight across the room, bouncing over the racetrack, bumping into the base of the HR-4, then slamming to a stop against the wall of the Mars simulator and toppling onto its side, revealing the go-cart-sized wheels at each corner, hidden by fabric flaps.

Hank's cheeks turned red. "A minor malfunction," he said. "I'm building that for a friend of mine to drive him around his home."

"Is he paralyzed?" I asked.

"No, just wealthy. And cosmically lazy. But the chair has been malfunctioning, unfortunately."

"May I take a look?" Ava asked.

Hank shrugged. "Be my guest."

Matt pointed up at the platforms. "How do you get up there?" he asked.

Hank brightened. "I'm glad you asked! There are ladders, of course, but I'm developing a much more efficient system." He pointed to the catapult, then tapped the screen of his smartphone a few times. A few seconds later the catapult sprang upright, launching the mannequin into the air. The human-shaped doll flew, flipped, and slammed its stomach against the edge of a platform. Hank winced as his test pilot dropped five stories and crashed onto the top of a steel cabinet in the middle of the room.

No one spoke.

"How disappointing," Hank said at last. "The last time, that worked perfectly."

Before one of us could reply, the birds overhead began screeching louder and louder. Something shattered. Hank threw out his arms, pushing us back, and one of the drones plummeted from the ceiling with a whoosh. The robot hit the floor and exploded into a hundred fragments of plastic and metal and circuitry.

Ava gasped.

Hank lifted the drivable chair back onto its wheels and flopped onto the cushioned seat. He leaned forward, resting his forehead on the heels of his hands. "I can't do it all alone," he said. "There's just too much."

"Too much what?" I asked.

The chair started moving. Startled, he grabbed the arms.

"Sorry!" Ava said, typing on the keyboard. "I'll switch it off."

Hank jumped to his feet and waved his hands all around. "Too much everything! Too many inventions to perfect. Too many devices to test."

"Why don't you hire assistants?" Matt asked.

Hank smiled.

"What?" Matt said.

"That, Matthew, is precisely what I wanted to talk to you about! In the past, my assistants were a great help. Absolutely. I was far more productive and focused. But they were always running off and taking my ideas with them. My last assistant stole one of my designs and sold it for nearly a million dollars. Granted, that's not a lot of money—"

"That's not a lot of money?" I asked.

"Oh, no, this idea was worth at least ten," Hank said.

Ava kicked me lightly on the ankle. Was I drooling? Possibly.

The HR-4 dinged. I flinched and raised my hands, ready to swat away any flying dough.

Matt said, "So, you were saying . . ."

"Let's eat first," Hank suggested. The robot opened the door on its chest, pulled out a perfectly cooked pizza, and hurled it at Hank like a cheese-covered Frisbee. Our dinner skimmed the top of his head, landed on an otherwise empty

39

steel table, and spun to a stop. Hank wiped the crust dust off his head and inspected our meal. He shrugged, removed a knife from a drawer, and sliced the pizza into irregular squares. "Now, where were we?"

"Assistants," Matt said, grabbing a slice.

Hank was watching me. I must have been wincing. "Go ahead, Jack. Coincidentally I sterilized this tabletop for an experiment earlier today. It's probably cleaner than your average dinner plate."

I picked up a thin slice. "Go on," I said.

"Okay, so here's the deal," Hank said. "I consulted with Min—"

The three of us shot one another panicked glances. "You talked to Min?" I said.

He waved his hands in front of his face. "No, no, don't worry. I wasn't reporting you for anything. She is a very charming woman, though. Very bright." He stared past us. The hint of a smile formed on his face.

"Uh . . . Hank?"

"What? Oh, right. So, you see, I spoke to her, and as you can tell, I need some help around the lab . . ."

"You need a lot of help," Ava said. She nodded to the busted robotic bird, then waved over at the junk pile. "Why do you even have a snowblower in here?"

Eyes raised, Hank rocked his head back and forth like

the second hand of an old-fashioned clock. "It's a long story, and, okay, sure, maybe I do need a lot of help. But I think you three might be up to the task. Ava, you are clearly a very talented engineer. Your drone—"

"Fred," she cut in. "His name is Fred."

"Well, he is truly impressive. Min showed me a video of that skateboard you built, too—"

"Pedro," I noted.

Hank laughed. "Pedro, eh? Clever. Anyway, I wonder if you could help me out with my birds, the chair, and the HR-4."

"Harry," Ava said.

"You think I should call it Harry?"

"Machines are people, too. They need real names."

"Right. Okay. Harry. That works." Hank drummed his fingers on his chin, then pointed at my brother. "Matthew, I really, really like the way you step back and think through problems. You're an observer! That is so, so critical. We can't form good theories without data, you know. I can't say I would've tasted the self-cleaning coating on the windows, and I do hope you didn't have any stomach problems the next day, but I was impressed, and I hadn't even thought of the security application. It did stop Jack, here, didn't it? Oh, and discovering my mail chute was a nice little feat, as well. And then that whole rabbit-warren concept—"

41

"You heard all that?" Matt asked. "Were you eavesdropping on us?"

"Not at the time, no. I wasn't actually here when you first visited. But one of my security cameras played back the video later, and I was very impressed with the way you thought your way through the problem, Matthew. I need someone who can help me bounce around ideas, circumvent obstacles, maybe even cook up a few projects. Do you think you could do that?"

Matt's effort to stifle his smile was failing miserably. He might as well have started jumping up and down and clapping. "I can try," he said.

"Good," Hank said. "Of course, there is also less glorious work to be done. Errands need to be run. Mail sorted. And then there are phones and e-mails to answer."

He didn't look at me. Neither did my siblings. But I could guess who would be left with those less-thrilling chores. And from the ridiculously large smiles on their faces, I could tell that my brother and sister were not going to walk away from this opportunity. In their heads, they were already on the job. But I still had a question. "Okay, so how much do you pay?" I asked. We had enough money from investing what remained of our poetry earnings. But still, who works for free?

"Pay?" Hank smiled; he thought I was joking. And Ava

and Matt laughed right along with him, ruining any chance we might have at a respectable salary. "Good one, Jack. Very clever. I spoke with your friend Min, and she thought you would benefit from my guidance. She said it could be an alternative education. Of course, there's no guarantee it will work. What I propose is a two-week trial period. What do you think? Two weeks, and then we'll decide whether to continue."

Before I even had time to take a deep breath, Ava and Matt shouted with excitement. Neither of them noticed that there was nothing in this arrangement to benefit me. But at least it was just going to be a trial.

# 3

# THE CLUTTERBUCK PRIZE

**T**HE TEST WAS OVER WITHIN A WEEK. WE PASSED. OR my siblings did, at least. I was dragged along for the ride, and six months later I was ready to quit. No, I was going to quit.

Ava, however, was pretty much in heaven. The drivable recliner was working beautifully, and with Hank's help she had upgraded it so that you could steer simply by leaning in whatever direction you wanted to go. She'd outfitted Fred with new motors and fans. Her little drone was now doing flips and pirouettes, and she was also building her own robotic submarine. She planned to call it Shelly, and she was hoping it could dive to depths of two hundred feet. Matt couldn't have been happier, either. He spent most of his time at the lab talking through some new problem with Hank, but he was also working on the Mars Simulator, the robotic legs, and more. The catapult still wasn't safe, and Harry couldn't reliably cook a pizza, but the robot no longer threw them at anyone, either. Overall, the geniuses were a success. The only thing that bugged my brother about our situation was that Hank still called him Matthew. I was pretty proud of that.

And sure, I was mildly proud of my work in the lab, too. The place was downright beautiful. Although it had been somewhat organized already, now the floors and table-tops were always clean and clear of clutter. When it came to errands, I was masterful. The old couple at the Laundromat knew me by name. Same with the guys at the electronics supply store. In less than fifteen minutes, I could fetch a double cappuccino from Hank's favorite coffee shop and carry it four blocks without losing any of the frothy milk. (The trick was taking a few sips through a straw, but don't tell him that.) Answering Hank's e-mails was probably the worst of my chores. Half of them I didn't even understand, and I had to ask Matt to scan them to see if they might be important. But I managed to keep the job interesting by occasionally writing back to people and telling them they'd reached the wrong address. I pretended to be a florist in rural Michigan. One guy even placed an order for a dozen roses.

Hank was constantly going on about what a great addition Ava and Matt were to the lab. And we certainly didn't slow him down. The guy never slept and never stopped. He was always working on ten projects at once, traveling

45

all over the world. He'd be in Moscow one week, Shanghai the next. He even had a trip to Antarctica planned.

Basically everyone was happy but me. I'd turned into a twelve-year-old secretary and housekeeper. Not that there's anything wrong with those jobs. It's just that I had bigger things in mind. A leading role in a blockbuster. An NBA contract. (I planned to grow.) Even a job running a small country would have been fine. But table sorter? E-mail answerer? No, thank you. On top of all that, I'd lost both my Xbox controllers, so I didn't even have gaming to get me through the day.

So now I was going to tell Hank that I was finished.

On a Friday afternoon in November, I sat down to write him a letter. Ava was hammering away at something on the other side of the lab. I couldn't concentrate, so I tried one of Hank's tricks. A few weeks earlier I'd noticed that whenever he was really deep into a project, he'd wear Birkenstock sandals, listen to jazz, and tap out miniature drum solos on his jaw, using his fingertips as sticks. I didn't like sandals. The finger drumming was a little weird. But the music was actually kind of cool, so I slipped on my headphones, chose one of Hank's jazz playlists, and grabbed a pen. I hadn't even gotten to "Dear," when Hank dropped into the seat across from me.

"What are you writing?" he asked.

I mumbled and stuttered.

He knocked his fist on the table a few times, then held up his index finger and pointed at me. "You know, I've been thinking about you, Jack."

"You have?"

"I have! Not much, I'll admit. Just a little. But in that little bit of thinking I came to the conclusion that you must be bored out of your skull in here. Am I right?"

After a pause I nodded.

"So, I think I told you already, but I'm heading to Antarctica on Sunday."

"You didn't."

"No?"

"No, but I read about it in your e-mails. The Clutterbuck Prize, right?"

"That's right," he said.

The billionaire J. F. Clutterbuck—the genius inventor of the hugely popular odorless sock—had launched an annual contest designed to address the world's biggest problems. Ridding the world of smelly footwear was not enough for Mr. Clutterbuck. He was determined to fight pollution, hunger, and more. The way his contest worked was fairly simple. He announced the goal, and the designs were due within one year. There was a demonstration of the entries, and whoever had invented the machine or system that best dealt with the particular problem would win a million dollars.

Hank judged the contests for Mr. Clutterbuck, so we'd all heard about the previous winners. A lady in South Korea won the antipollution prize for a device that pulled plastic out of the ocean. A scientist in Minnesota won the feed-the-hungry contest with a system that recycled leftovers into healthy meals. I wasn't too impressed with that one, though. Hank had one of the prototypes at the lab. To me it made everything taste like a combination of meat loaf, cashew nuts, and those gauze pads dentists jam into your mouth after pulling a tooth.

48

The most recent contest, which I'd read about in Hank's e-mails, challenged inventors to come up with a better way to filter the salt out of ocean water so it would be safe to drink. I hadn't known it, but apparently hundreds of millions of people don't have access to clean drinking water. They're forced to drink stuff that's filthy and filled with germs. The water-cleansing inventions designed for the latest Clutterbuck Prize were all going to be tested down in Antarctica. What I hadn't been able to figure out was why they'd chosen such a remote spot. "Why Antarctica?" I asked. "Couldn't you get them to send you someplace more fun? Like Tahiti?"

"Huge shortage of drinking water down at the bottom of

the world," Hank explained. "They get all their water from an expensive and completely inefficient machine. It's really the perfect place to test a new one. Plus, I've always wanted to go, so I talked J. F. into the idea. As a bonus, another friend of mine is doing research down there this season. She said she's had some groundbreaking findings."

"Anna Donatelli, right?"

His eyebrows rose. "How did you know?"

That was the name on the envelope we found the day we tried to retrieve Fred. Plus, Hank had received a burst of messages from her recently. "Her e-mails," I said. "She adds the weirdest emojis at the bottom."

"Anna's a very strange and rare bird. You'd like her."

I wasn't sure if I should be flattered or offended.

His stare drifted toward the ceiling, and I waited until I was certain he was finished talking. "That should be fun for you," I said at last.

"It will be! Amazing fun. Antarctica is a real scientific paradise." He knocked on the table again. Then he leaned forward and whispered, "I think you should come with me."

"Me?" I tried to look cool but couldn't help smiling. "Really? Me?"

"All three of you."

Of course he meant all three of us. I don't know why I'd thought otherwise. Over Hank's shoulder, on the far side of

49

the lab, I could see Ava and Matt staring up at the robotic birds circling high overhead. The geniuses still hadn't figured out what was wrong with them. Typically they lost a bird a week.

"Did you ask them?"

Hank leaned back and held up both his hands. "No, I'm asking you," he said. "School won't be a problem, right?" I shrugged; we could follow our assignments online. "The beauty of homeschooling. Your home could be anywhere. So, what do you say? You make the decision on this one, Jack. You lead. Should the four of us spend a few weeks down at the South Pole together?"

I didn't say anything. But apparently I didn't need to.

"You're smiling. Is that a yes? Are you in?"

"Well, I mean, it does sound like a lot of work, and since you're not paying us, how about a little bonus?" I asked. "Maybe a nice big gift card?"

Hank laughed and slapped the table. "You can't put a price on an experience like this one!"

I disagreed, but before I could respond, he yelled out the news of our trip to the others. They were puzzled at first, as any kid would be if an adult were to yell out, "We're going to the South Pole!" But once Hank explained the situation, they didn't need much convincing.

"What do we get to bring?" Ava asked.

"Bring? What do you mean? Clothes, of course. Winter gear—"

"No, no, no," she said. "I mean, which projects."

"You should bring Shelly, plus anything else you think might prove useful. I already sent a few larger items down ahead of us."

Matt peeked over his shoulder, then sighed with relief. "Not the catapult, though. Good."

"The catapult? Ha, no. Although I imagine penguins might enjoy that."

"So, what did you send?" Ava asked.

"Well, you see, the South Pole isn't very kind to machines. I'd like to see whether the robolegs can operate in such frigid conditions, for example. I'm planning to test a few other applications, as well, including a little surprise I've been working on in my spare time."

"A surprise?" Ava asked.

"You don't have spare time," I noted.

"True! None of us does. Life is too short. Anyway, we'll have plenty of time to talk later. Go. You need to start packing. In fact, come to think of it, so do I."

Matt and Ava bolted off to different parts of the lab. I grabbed my backpack and stuffed in a few essentials from the Clutterbuck table, including the nose vacuum and the self-drying boxers. Then we hurried home. On our way back

51

to the apartment, Matt kept going on about how parts of Antarctica resembled distant planets and moons. Practically everything he said started with "Did you know . . ." And I didn't. And it really got annoying.

What thrilled Matt most of all was the strange world under the ice-covered seas. "That's what Anna Donatelli's work is all about," he said. "She looks for creatures under the ice." He held up a huge stack of papers. "Hank printed out all her research for me. Plus pretty much every interview she's ever done."

Ava reached over and thumbed through the pile. "Kind of a waste of paper, even if it is recycled," Ava said.

"Reading printouts is easier on the eyes," Matt explained.

Once home, Ava began trying to crowd her whole workshop into her bag. Hank had suggested bringing extra batteries for Fred and Shelly, since the power sources wouldn't last long in the frigid air, so she grabbed every one she could find. I had to remind her that she couldn't pack only electronics. We'd need clothes down there at the bottom of the world, too. You know, maybe even a toothbrush? But she wasn't listening. As for me, I'd learned how to pack from my third foster father, the same guy who'd introduced me to coffee. He'd been in the navy—very briefly—and he'd showed me how to roll each item of clothing tightly, then stuff them into your bag one by one. He also showed me how to steal certain cars, which is why we didn't last long as a team. Anyway, my pack was only half full by the time I'd jammed in all I needed, so I snuck into Ava's room when she wasn't looking, grabbed a few extra items of clothing for her, and added them to my bag. Just in case. I was halfway out the door when I decided that this opportunity was way too nice to pass up. So I swapped in clothes I knew she hated, including a pink fleece jacket she refused to wear because she was "no princess," and a pair of Hello Kitty sweatpants. I may not be as brilliant as my siblings, but I'm a genius at annoying them.

A little after nine on Sunday morning, a long black car pulled up in front of our apartment stoop. We were all red-eyed and bleary. Not one of us had slept. And when the back door swung open, Hank didn't look too fantastic, either. He stepped out wearing Birkenstock sandals. The car stereo was playing jazz with a lot of mumbling in the background, so I guessed it was this musician named Keith Jarrett. He's one of Hank's favorites and he makes weird noises when he plays. Clearly Hank had been working hard and sleeping little. You would've thought an invisible puppeteer was hiding above him somewhere, holding his eyelids open and trying to pull his mouth into a smile. "Morning," he managed. "Who's ready for a little vacation to the most desolate and extreme place on the planet?"

53

"When you put it that way, I'm in!" Ava said. Holding her bag with both arms, she bounded into the wide backseat.

The driver sped us out to a small airport in New Jersey, where a private jet awaited us on the runway. A dented red Honda was parked at the foot of the rollaway stairs. We knew the vehicle. And the driver. Ava ran out to greet her when we stopped. "You're coming with us?" she asked.

Small and thin, with straight jet-black hair and greenish-brown eyes, Min was scowling. Hank stumbled out of the car. "No," she said, "I'm not going with you. What were you thinking, Hank?"

"You said I should do something nice for them," Hank said, his words separated by yawns, "to show my appreciation. You said they haven't traveled much, so I thought—"

"I meant, get them a present!" Min said. "Or, if you were going to take them somewhere, Disney World would have been more appropriate."

"I'd prefer the South Pole," Matt said.

"Me, too," I added. In truth, though, I wasn't really sure. I'd never actually been to Disney.

"They're not going," Min said, still staring at Hank.

"Wait," Ava said. "What do you mean?"

Matt and I hurled several questions of our own at her.

"This is completely irresponsible," she said. "Antarctica

54

is one of the most dangerous places on Earth. And you're children!"

"Not legally," I noted.

"Jack's right," Hank said.

Min practically stuck her tongue out at me. For an adult she could do a really good impression of a six-year-old. "Physically they are," she said, "and that's what matters here."

I couldn't really let that go. "Well, actually, what matters is the legal—"

"Hank'll take care of us," Matt said.

Eyebrows raised, Min replied, "Does he look like he's going to be able to take care of anyone right now?"

Hank yawned again. This time his eyes did not re-open.

55

"He just had a late night," Ava said.

"Look at him! One of you is practically going to have to carry him down there."

As Hank started to crumple from exhaustion, Matt looped an arm around his back and held him up easily. "Not a problem. He's actually kind of light."

Now Hank straightened and rubbed his face. He tapped the side of his head. "That's because of all my lofty ideas."

Min sighed. "I can't even—"

"We're going," Ava said.

"Please," I added. "Trust us. We can handle ourselves."

"Up here, sure," she said. "But from everything I've read, it's a different world down there. Brutal. Hostile."

"We'll figure it out," Matt said.

Hank held his hands together in front of his chest. "They'll be fine. I give you my word. And I'll send you regular updates."

Min closed her eyes and shook her head. Then she flicked her fingers in the direction of the jet. "Well, at least you'll be starting the journey in style. Whose plane is this, anyway?"

"Clutterbuck's!" Hank answered, already on his way up the rollaway stairs. "And the chef is amazing."

"So, we can go?" Ava asked.

"As Jack said, I can't really stop you."

Ava gave Min a quick, stiff hug, then pointed a thumb at the aircraft. "There's a chef in there?"

"Apparently," Min said. She pitched her head forward and stared at me. "Are you sure you know what you're in for?"

"Of course," I answered. I'd skimmed Wikipedia the night before. And I almost watched a documentary about Antarctica, too. But the narrator had this really sleepy accent, so my eyes closed during the opening credits. "It'll be fine."

As Ava started up the stairs, Min passed me a canvas bag full of books. "These might help you prepare," she said.

The top book was hardbound in blue cloth. The title, lettered in faded gold, read *A Field Guide to the Frozen Frontier*. "Are they all about Antarctica?"

Min nodded. Then she put a hand on my shoulder and leaned in. "I know it's hard trying to keep up with those two, Jack. But even if you don't feel like you can outthink them"—she reached forward and tapped the book cover—"you can always outread them."

"Thanks," I murmured.

Min shooed me up the stairs. "Just be careful," she said. "Promise me that you'll be careful."

# 4

# THE BOTTOM OF
# THE WORLD

**S**O THERE'S COFFEE. AND THEN THERE'S COFFEE ON A private jet. When Jen, our hostess, took our drink orders, she kept trying to push me toward chocolate milk or ginger ale. She even offered a root beer float. But I knew what I wanted. Hank was snoring like a baby bear, so he couldn't explain my obsession with the black gold. But it goes back to my third foster father, who used to wake me up before sunrise to drink a small, sugary cup with him at the wobbly kitchen table. Since then I'd been kind of hooked. I assured Jen that I was perfectly accustomed to drinking a cup.

"Kids shouldn't drink coffee," she said.

"It's healthier than an energy drink."

Matt tapped rapidly on his iPad, then showed Jen the screen. I didn't have to look to know that Matt had just dug up a scientific research paper or two that backed my claim. This was a galactically annoying habit when he used it against me, but not when Matt was on my side. "He's right," my brother said. "Here's the research if you want to read it."

The expression on Jen's face was a wordless "whatever." "You kids sure are something," she said, and not in a complimentary kind of way. "Keep the research. What kind of coffee would you like?" she asked me.

"What do you have?"

A slightly devious smile flashed across Jen's face. "I have the perfect cup for you, made from very rare and expensive civet beans."

Ten minutes later, the billionaire's version of my favorite drink was set down on the mahogany table in front of me. On a private jet, coffee does not arrive in a simple paper cup. It floats out of the galley on a silver tray, swimming in a porcelain cup. A separate porcelain container of fresh milk stands beside it, along with a silver bowl neatly packed with cubes of both brown and white sugar. I thanked Jen, prepared my cup with great care, sipped gently, and sighed with pleasure.

"You are so lame," Ava said, sucking down her third ginger ale. Then she glanced back at Hank, who was still snoring, and leaned toward my seat. She was trying not to smile. I could guess what she wanted to talk about. She'd mentioned her theory before. "Don't you think it's weird?"

"Not again, Ava."

59

"Seriously, though. How does Min know so much about Hank? Why does he even listen to her? They're totally dating."

"Hey, what's that?" I asked, pointing out the window. Ava turned, and I pressed the emergency call button on her armrest. As Jen hustled from the galley to see what was wrong, I collected my books and my drink and found a new seat in the spacious plane. Ava tried to blame me for the hostess's alarm, but the victory was mine.

Now, back to that coffee. The drink was essential, because I couldn't afford to sleep. I was determined to finish *A Field Guide to the Frozen Frontier* and skim a few of the books about Antarctica's early explorers before we arrived. When my boots stepped down onto that ice, I wanted to be an expert on the place. Or at least know more about it than Matt and Ava did. And I certainly had time. The trip was going to take four flights and nearly three days.

First, though, I opened my laptop and skimmed through the e-mails from Hank's scientist friend Anna Donatelli. Besides the unusual emojis, which included cartoon versions of a dancing elephant seal and a penguin playing a harmonica, what stood out was the intensity of her messages. She was all but begging Hank to get down there, and she wasn't afraid to use exclamation points. "You have to see what I've found! Fly down immediately! No, sooner. Please!!

This is bigger than science!!!!!" Once Hank informed her that he was on his way, Anna Donatelli's reply contained no words at all. She sent back an e-mail packed with twenty-four exclamation points—I counted—and seven dancing seals. For all her excitement, though, she didn't offer any real clues to what she'd actually discovered, and before long I closed my laptop and switched to the books Min had given me.

When that first flight was over, they pretty much had to peel me out of my seat on Clutterbuck's jet. Our hostess actually gave me a small bag of the civet coffee beans to take with me, and for  some reason she was wearing that devious smile again. The next plane was hardly so luxurious, and our rides became less comfortable each time we switched. In New Zealand, as we left the tiny terminal to head toward the runway for our last flight, a man with a ruddy face and droopy eyes stopped us just past the exit. Behind him was a huge cart stuffed with red, fur-lined jackets. He grimaced when he saw us— Hank had warned us that some people weren't thrilled that he was bringing kids to the South Pole—then pulled two coats from the very bottom of the bin and handed them to Ava and me. "Go ahead," he said, "try 'em on."

The breeze was warm, and the sun was hot on the back

61

of my neck, so it felt strange to be testing a coat designed for extreme cold. But in a few hours we were going to land in one of the most frigid places on the planet. So I zipped up. The jacket wasn't just warm; it felt like I was snuggling with a family of friendly bears. The smallest size was still a little too large, but it would work for me and Ava.

"That's your 'Big Red'—your expedition parka," the man said. "She'll be your best friend down there on the ice— and up there in your plane. She keeps every- thing out. And everything in," he added, winking at me.

There is a secret language between males of the human species that I speak quite well. So with great care I let one out. Then I waited. I knew from the heat, and the several bags of chocolate cookies I'd gobbled down on the last flight, that I'd released something strong. Yet no scent arose to my nostrils. Not even a whiff. "Nice," I said.

"Isn't it?" the man agreed.

Matt's jacket fit perfectly, but Hank mumbled some- thing about wishing his could be taken in at the shoulders. Wrapped in our Big Reds, the four of us followed the two dozen or so other passengers onto the runway and up the rollaway stairs. Our actual destination in Antarctica was McMurdo Station, a United States government research center. So for this last portion of the trip we'd be riding in a massive US Air Force cargo plane. I wasn't expecting private-jet-style comfort and service, but this mechanical bird was built to carry tanks, not people. Picture an enormous metal tube with two huge wings and four giant propellers. All the passengers had to cram into metal seats with straight backs; our Big Reds were the only cushions. Most people pulled their hoods over their faces and prepared to sleep.

"This should be fun," Ava said, rolling her eyes.

"Loads of it," Matt added.

The plane shook like a washing machine on spin cycle and sounded like the world's largest blow-dryer, and we hadn't even started moving yet. A woman sitting across the aisle from us was staring at Hank. "Are you—"

"He is," Ava answered. "Would you like his autograph?"

"No," she said, as if this were the most ridiculous question she'd ever been asked.

Hank had already begun to reach into his jacket for a pen, but he moved his hand to his shoulder instead, pretending to massage a sore spot. "Are you a scientist?" Hank asked the woman.

"I'm a firefighter," she answered.

"Why are firefighters needed on an ice world?" Ava asked.

63

I nearly jumped out of my seat; I'd just read all about this in the book. "I know!" I said. "On the base there's always a risk of a fire, and you also need firefighters for rescue missions, emergencies, people getting lost out on the ice or caught in a storm. There's a whole population of people down there who have nothing to do with science. Cooks and engineers and truck drivers and even shopkeepers. They keep the base running."

"Not bad," the woman said.

"I'm Jack," I said, holding my hand out to her across the aisle.

The woman shoved her hand into her fur-lined pocket instead. "And I'm going to sleep," she said. "See you on Ross."

"That's short for Ross Island, home of McMurdo Station," I explained to Ava.

"I know that, and I'm going to sleep, too."

There were a thousand other things I wanted to tell Ava and Matt about Antarctica. First of all, it's as large as the United States, not counting Alaska, and 98 percent of it is ice. If the whole thing were a pizza, and you cut the pie into a hundred slices, all but two would be frozen. In the summer, the sun never sets. It just kind of circles around the horizon, rising higher, then dipping lower, never quite disappearing. And in the winter it's all darkness, all the time.

I have an irrational but serious fear of vampires, so I was glad we were going in early summer. The way I see it, if vampires really do exist, those dark Antarctic winters would be ideal for their vacations.

Even though it's brighter than the winter, summer in Antarctica isn't exactly pleasant. They have a different idea of good weather down there. If you don't have to cover your face to protect it from instant frostbite, that's a lovely day. Fifteen degrees Fahrenheit is toasty, even though it's below freezing. A bad storm is when the temperature is under a hundred degrees below zero, the wind is blowing at fifty-five knots, and you can't see anything in front of you because of all the snow whipping around. They call that kind of storm a "Herbie." You don't want to get caught outside in a Herbie.

Our destination, McMurdo Station, sounded kind of cool. About a thousand people lived and worked there in the summer, a few hundred in the winter. In addition to the various science labs and sleeping dorms, the research center boasts a bowling alley, a basketball court, a movie theater, and a rock-climbing wall. All indoors, of course. It even has a coffee shop.

What else? I'll run through the highlights. They call the common cold down there "the crud." There's a huge volcano, Mount Erebus, which shoots out lava that freezes instantly, turning into crystals.

65

Then there were the early Antarctic explorers. Those dudes were completely brutal. One group of them actually ate penguins to survive. Honestly. They turned cute little penguins into steaks. Seal soup was also a popular item on their menus.

During another famous expedition, the team began their journey to the South Pole with forty-eight dogs and returned with only a dozen.

On purpose.

Get it?

Exactly.

Even though it's frigid all the time in Antarctica, you can get sunburned and dehydrated. The cold can suck all the moisture out of your skin. The snow can blind you. And everybody is supposed to stick to a set of crazy rules designed to make sure that humans don't mess the place up. So when you go on a field trip to explore, you have to carry little bottles and plastic bags with you to take care of your business. If you're lucky, you get to use a bucket with a Styrofoam seat. But sometimes you just have to ask your tent-mates to turn the other way.

And the ice itself? Well, the ice is so thick and solid in some places that you can land a cargo plane right down on the surface of it. Which is exactly what we were about to do in our giant metal bird. The tin-can plane dipped. Ava woke up, and through a window to our right we saw the white expanse of Antarctica. The whole world was reduced to two colors, blue and white. In the distance, Mount Erebus was like a cloud factory spewing vapor into the air.

"Planes might not be able to do this for much longer," Hank said.

"Do what?" Ava asked.

"Land on the ice."

"Why not?" Ava pressed.

"Global warming!" Hank said. "Climate change could melt this place."

The rattling, winged tube struck the icy runway, bumping along for a few seconds before settling into a glide. I was as rigid as a board. For a moment I pictured us slipping across the ice, out onto the edge, and plunging into the blue water, but we were miles from open ocean. I closed my eyes and did not open them again until the plane stopped, the huge cargo door opened, and a blast of icy wind practically punched me in the face.

"Whoa!" Hank said. "That'll wake you up! Look at those bluebird skies. And the ice . . . notice its bluish tinge? In the height of the summer this entire ice shelf will be completely melted. Imagine that!"

Outside, everything was white and blue and impossibly bright. My eyes burned from the light reflecting off the

67

snow and ice. Squinting barely helped, and the air was like a giant frozen hand wrapping around my chest. We climbed out of the plane, and at the bottom of the metal stairs, Matt tripped. He landed in the snow and slid forward.

And it was awesome.

Once Matt was on his feet again, with the snow brushed off his scarlet parka but the red in his face still glowing,  we crossed the ice and headed for McMurdo's version of a taxi, a beastly red vehicle named Ivan the Terra Bus. Only Ivan wasn't like any kind of taxi or bus I'd ever seen. A big red metal box sitting atop giant wheels, it looked like a cross between a garbage truck and a broken-down space freighter from a science-fiction movie. I half expected a crowd of small hooded aliens to scurry out of the back and try to start selling us scrap electronics. Instead, a half-dozen humans emerged and began welcoming and waving us inside.

A woman wearing a green woolen hat hurried up to Hank. "Dr. Witherspoon! Such a pleasure. Really. I'm Britney Kirshner, one of the geoscientists here. Beautiful out, isn't it? The first time I arrived here, I felt like I'd just stepped onto the moon."

"Yes, it's spectacular, and call me Hank, please."

"Certainly," she said. Her eyes were bright blue, her

cheeks bright red. A few strands of reddish-brown hair hung down over her eyes. "I hope you'll do the same."

"You want him to call you Hank?" Ava asked.

"What? No. I want him to call me Britney. I . . . Oh, you were joking."

"She's quite the comedian," I said.

"Where's Anna?" Hank asked. "I'll admit, I expected her to meet us."

"No one told you?" Britney asked.

"No one told me what?"

"Anna has disappeared."

# 5
# DINING WITH THE ENEMY

**I** WANTED ANSWERS IMMEDIATELY. WHAT HAD HAPPENED? When did she disappear? Why? But Hank didn't appear concerned at all. He said Anna always liked to do things her own way. Years ago, they were in an African desert, hoping to find fossils in fallen meteorites, when Anna decided to walk back to their camp from the field site. Seventy miles. Through the desert. Without telling anyone. So he was certain this whole disappearing act was just Anna being Anna. When I pressed him with questions, he said we'd have plenty of time later to discuss everything. But we couldn't talk on the ride to McMurdo Station, because the rattling, rumbling truck was too loud. And we couldn't talk when we finally got to the base, because we were too busy filling out forms and meeting contestants for the Clutterbuck Prize and touring the buildings and getting lectured on rule after rule after rule. I didn't get my chance to ask any questions until we sat down at our table in the cafeteria.

Inside, there were several dozen long tables, the air smelled of cleaning fluids, and the food was nearly colorless. The green beans looked closer to brown. The carrots were more yellow than orange. I went with the plain beige buttered noodles and sat down across from Britney.

"Normally we don't dress up for dinner here," she said, eyeing my shirt and tie. "Are those . . . rockets on your bowtie?"

I nodded. "That's right."

Matt set his tray next to mine and nudged me aside a little. Britney laughed when she saw his plate piled high. "You should save room for Mr. Frosty," she said.

"Who's that?" Ava asked.

Britney pointed across the room to an antique soft-serve ice cream machine—a big square beauty with gleaming silver handles and white nozzles dripping with chocolate and vanilla. I had a strong feeling that Mr. Frosty and I were going to be very good friends. "Also, if you don't like what they're serving for dinner here, you can always order pizza. They deliver twenty-four hours a day."

This was very good news. Normally I would've asked about the quality of the pepperoni, but we had more important things to discuss. As everyone quietly dug into their meals, I set my fork down on my blue plastic tray. "Can we talk about Anna Donatelli now?" I asked Hank.

71

He shrugged. "Sure. What do you want to know?"

"What if something happened to her? What if she's in trouble?"

"Ignore him," Ava said to Britney.

"No, really," I continued. "Think about it. There's a mandatory buddy system here, right, Britney?"

"That's right," she said. "No one ever goes out alone."

"Exactly! So she wouldn't have been allowed to. It's against the rules."

"It's a lab, not a prison," Hank said. "And Anna's never had much regard for rules."

"Which is not the way for anyone to operate down here," Britney said, pausing between her words for emphasis. She stared briefly at Ava and Matt, then fixed her eyes on me for a few beats longer. "The rules of McMurdo are in place for a reason. You understand that?"

Her tone and expression were graveyard serious.

"Yes. Totally. We understand," I insisted. "But getting back to Anna . . . doesn't it seem odd," I asked Hank, "that she'd take off right before our arrival? She was all excited for you to come down here." I pictured the reply with twenty-four exclamation points. "Then she just disappears? That's like throwing a party for yourself and then leaving before it starts."

"I've done that," Hank said with a laugh. "My fortieth

birthday, if I recall correctly. Right before the party started, I was struck by the notion that my age was irrelevant, and . . ." Hank squirmed as he noticed Matt chewing with his mouth open. As a favor to us, he tried not to scold us in front of others when our table manners failed. There was a code word for each of us; Matt's referred to one of the moons of Mars. "Phobos, Matthew. Please."

My brother blushed, closed his mouth, and resumed chewing.

There was a commotion at the table next to us; a tall man spat out his coffee in disgust, declaring that it tasted like dishwater.

Britney leaned forward and whispered, "He's right. The coffee here is revolting."

That news hurt. I felt like I hadn't slept in weeks, and I'd been hoping for a decent cup. But this was no time to worry about the quality of McMurdo's coffee beans. "Back to Anna," I said. "Do you know her, Britney?"

"I do," she said. "We've become good friends, in fact. The first day we met, I was sitting right where you are now, Ava, and I saw this woman rearranging the pile of cafeteria trays at the counter. She sat down across from me after she got her food. I asked what she'd been doing, and she said the trays hadn't been stacked correctly. She said disorder bothered her."

Hank nodded. "Anna is painfully neat," he admitted. "Very, very organized."

"I wouldn't want her to see my workbench," Ava said.

I nodded at Britney. "What else?"

Staring at the ceiling, Hank answered instead. "I seem to recall that she doesn't like peas. Of course, there is also her research, which is phenomenal. Right, Matthew?" My brother was clearly desperate to spit out what he'd learned, but his mouth was too full, so Hank continued talking. "Do you work with Anna?"

Britney held up a finger, then finished chewing. "No," she said after a breath. "I study sea-ice interactions."

Thankfully, Ava said what I was thinking. "What?"

Our new friend held one hand flat above the table, then pushed her fist up against the outstretched fingers. "Let's say my right fist is a freshwater iceberg, and my left hand is the ocean surface. I study the places where they collide."

I yawned. "Sorry," I said.

Matt backhanded me on the shoulder.

"Don't worry about it," Britney said. "I get that it's not quite as exciting as Anna's research. Or not to you, at least. So, what do you think happened to her, Jack?" she asked with a smirk. "You think she was kidnapped or something?"

Her expression was annoying; she was looking at me like I was a second grader. "No, but I can't help wondering if disappearing wasn't her choice. What if someone forced her to flee the base? Did she owe anybody money or anything?"

Ava reached across the table and laid her palm flat on the surface in front of Britney. "Really, I'm sorry about our brother. He reads way too much."

"There's no such thing as reading too much." The legs of her chair creaked as Britney pushed back from the table. "Besides, I'm intrigued, Jack. I'll play your game."

One other player was all I needed. But where to start? I thought for a moment. "So, Hank, in her e-mails she said she'd discovered something big, right?"

"She's prone to grand proclamations," Hank answered, "but she was quite adamant that this was a major find. She said it was even bigger than science."

75

"Nothing is bigger than science," Matt said. He looked to Hank for approval. He'd been doing that a lot lately. But Hank didn't notice.

"So let's say she did find something major," I pressed.

"Like what?" Ava asked. "What was she searching for?"

"Creatures," Matt said.

"What kind of creatures, you ask?" Hank said. Nobody actually asked, but that never stopped Hank. He tapped his boot on the linoleum. "Anna has spent decades searching the globe for new, extreme forms of life. She has scoured mountain peaks, deserts, coral reefs. This is her latest stop.

So, imagine that the floor here is the seafloor. Our table"—he gave the wooden surface a few knocks—"is a layer of ice. And everything in between?"

"Water," Ava said.

"Very, very cold water," Matt added.

"Right, exactly." Hank swept his hand across the table, accidentally knocking over a pepper shaker. "This wonderfully thick layer of ice covers the entire Ross Sea, between this island and mainland Antarctica." Now he moved his hand in a circle below the table. "Anna has long been interested in this hidden world between the ice and the seafloor. This is where she has been searching for new creatures. When she said she had a breakthrough, I guessed she'd found a new species."

"But she didn't say, right?" Matt asked.

"I heard she came back from her last expedition pretty excited," Britney said.

"When was that?" I asked.

"Monday. Then last night, Tuesday night, she disappeared."

"See?" Hank said, pointing at me. "She hasn't even been gone for a day!"

"Right, right," I said. "But what if she found something amazing, and someone wanted to steal it or something?"

"Scientists don't work that way," Hank said.

"Sure we do," Britney countered. "We're just as competitive as other humans."

"Was it you? Did you do it?" I asked.

Matt started to apologize for me. "Jack doesn't mean—"

"No, no, that's fair," Britney replied. "But I didn't have anything to do with Anna's disappearance."

"How do we know that?" Ava asked. Both Hank and Matt looked surprised that she was on my side.

"Three reasons. First, she's a woman. Female scientists are rare down here. We take care of each other. Second, Anna and I study completely different fields. I wouldn't have any reason to steal her work."

"And third?" I asked.

"I wasn't here," she said. "I was a hundred miles away. I got back right before you arrived."

"Those are pretty good answers," Ava said with a shrug.

I agreed. But I wasn't going to let Britney off completely. "Okay, so maybe you're not the lead suspect. But if not you, then who would want to harm Anna?"

Britney leaned back and looked around the room. "Golden?"

"Which one is he?" I asked.

She tipped her glass in the direction of a man with curly, shoulder-length blond hair that he tucked repeatedly behind his ears. A bright orange jacket was draped over the back of his chair. "His real name is Franklin Golding, but everyone calls him Golden because he's the golden boy. He's on the cover of a different science magazine every other month. He has found more strange forms of life down here than anyone. And he knows he's good. The guy won't even wear a Big Red like the rest of us. He has his own custom-made, bright orange jacket."

"I wonder if it fits better through the shoulders," Hank remarked.

A small, bearded man set a bowl of ice cream in front of Golding. The scientist didn't even thank him. I detested "Golden Boy" immediately. But that didn't make him guilty. "Who else?" I asked. "Was she working closely with anyone?"

"Levokin," Britney said. "But he always seemed kind of harmless to me."

"Levokin," Ava said. "Is that Russian?"

"Yes. Evgeny Levokin. He was part of the team that came down here with Anna."

"A Russian villain?" Matt said. "Isn't that a little too obvious?"

"Is he also a biologist?" I asked.

"More of an inventor, I'd say. He developed an amazing new wet suit for divers and researchers like Anna."

Hank was staring at the ceiling again. "Levokin, Levokin. The name is familiar. An inventor, you said? Yes,

yes. I believe he's competing for the Clutterbuck Prize this year."

"Whoa," Ava said. "Back up to the wet suit. Do people actually swim in this water?"

Hank pointed his fork at her. A noodle hung off the end. "That's one of the ways they explore the underwater world. They use small remote submarines, as well, so Shelly will fit right in, Ava, but human divers are essential. The problem is that they cannot dive for long because of the extreme cold."

"How do they even get down into the water, if it's frozen over?" Ava asked.

"In some cases, they drill holes through the ice shelf to access the water," Britney answered. "But sometimes there are naturally occurring holes that—"

"Seal holes, right?" Actually, I knew I was right; I'd read about them. I was just pretending to be humble. "Seals pop up through them to breathe. But the holes can close and freeze up again pretty quickly."

"Valenza!"

"Excuse me?" Hank said.

"Victor Valenza," Britney repeated, lowering her voice to a whisper. "He's been diving under the ice down here for ten years. A few times a year he even jumps in without a suit on, just for an instant, to show off. He'd have to be a suspect," she said to me. With one hand flat on the table, she raised her index finger and pointed at a dark-eyed, round man sitting on the other side of the room. His cheeks looked swollen. His gray hair was cut short, and one ear appeared to be slightly higher than the other. Either that or he was just leaning to one side.

"Why him?" I asked.

"He held all the diving records: most dives, longest dive, deepest dive . . . all of them. He was the best diver down here."

Ava turned her head slightly. "Was?"

"Until Anna," Britney said. "I heard this new wet suit Levokin designed is unbelievable. When she's wearing it, she can stay down longer and do more dives per day than Valenza would even dare—"

"Henry Witherspoon!"

A fine mist of spit settled on the back of my neck. I cringed, wiped it off with the sleeve of my hoodie, and turned. Behind me stood a man with a thick gray beard and gray-blond hair. He pronounced Hank's name "Weath-Aspin," and if he had a neck, it was fully retracted. He quickly sucked the tips of several of his fingers, wiped them on his shirt, then held out a huge red hand that smelled vaguely like honey.

Hank waved. There was no way he was going to touch the man's hand. "Please, call me Hank. And you are . . . ?"

"Daniel Perkins. Danno. I manage the desalination plant, mate. I'm going for that Clutterbuck Prize with my DP-1000. She could pull the salt out of all the world's oceans if we needed her to."

"Well, I don't think that will be necessary, Mr. Perkins, but of course I'll consider your DS-1000 as closely as I do all the other contest entries."

"D*P*," he said. "D*P*-1000. It's ten percent more efficient than anything out there. Ten percent!"

In the history of awkward silences, the one that followed was not the longest, but it would have to rank as one of the most intense. Hank's face paled. I considered knocking my water glass over onto Matt's tray to break the tension. Thankfully, Britney ended our social pain. "I'd finish up your meals so you can get some sleep," she said. "You guys have a big week ahead. You start field training tomorrow."

"Don't forget Sunday," Danno added.

"Sunday?" Hank asked.

"The day you'll be announcing the winner of the Clutterbuck Prize."

Hank yawned. "Right. Of course."

Danno nodded at Britney. "So, are they going to be happy campers?"

Did he think we were five years old? I shook my head at Ava. Britney must have noticed. "'Happy Camper School' is another name for the field training program," she explained. The moment she said that, I remembered it from my reading. "It might feel nice and cozy inside here, but the world outside these walls is frigid, harsh, and completely unfit for humans. It's one of the most dangerous places on the planet."

"Without Happy Camper training," Danno added, "you wouldn't survive an hour out there. You'd be ice cubes."

He was grinning. And I tried to return the expression. But what he'd said was light-years from funny. I gulped. As I stared down at the remains of my noodles, I started wondering if Min had been right. Maybe Disney would have been a better choice.

# 6
# SOME KIND OF TROUBLE

O I KNOW BRITNEY RECOMMENDED THAT WE REST, and I was beyond exhausted from all those flights, but sleep just wasn't happening. On our way out of the dining room, two British scientists had asked Hank a question about climate change. That was like dangling a juicy worm in front of a starved bluefish. Hank couldn't resist snapping up the bait. As he started to talk, Matt stayed to listen, but I grabbed Ava's elbow and hustled her into the hallway.

"What's the rush?" she asked.

"We have a little mission."

She stopped and held up her hands. "I'm not getting kicked out of here on the first night."

"You're not getting kicked out. Besides, they can't just send us home. We're in Antarctica."

"So what are we doing, then?"

"Research. That's all."

"That's all?"

No, of course not. But I was getting there. "We're going to check out Anna's room. To see if she left any clues that could tell us where she went."

Around the corner we nearly walked into a tall woman with long silvery hair. She sneered. "You two."

Ava held up a hand and flashed her brightest smile. "Hi! I'm Ava."

"Don't try to charm me, princess," the woman snapped. "Where's the other one?"

The battery powering Ava's smile died.

"He's with Mr. Witherspoon," I said. "Excuse me, ma'am, but why are you looking for our brother?"

"Don't call me ma'am. I am the director of this base, so you can call me Director, Your Highness, Respected Leader. But I would prefer that you not call me anything at all. I would prefer that our paths never cross again, in fact. They never should have let you three onto my island. And this Clutterbuck Prize? It's ridiculous! An insult to real scientists."

"Desalination is real science," Ava protested.

I could hear the director grinding her teeth. "Do not talk. Right now your only job is to listen. I am looking and will continue to look for every possible reason to put you children and your friend back on the next plane to wherever it is that you came from. So I urge you to remain on your absolute best behavior. Understood?"

Ava elbowed me to make sure I didn't blurt out a rude response. The two of us nodded, agreeing to the woman's terms.

"Good," the director said. "Now go find a coloring book or something. The very sight of you rattles my bones."

We waited until the sound of her footsteps faded. "I'm not a princess," Ava muttered. Her left eyebrow rose higher than its neighbor. "Coloring books? Really?"

"Forget it," I said. "Let's get back to finding Anna's room."

"Fine," Ava said. "Any idea where it might be?"

"Well, that's where your brilliance comes in. I don't actually know." If I could've figured out that answer on my own, I wouldn't have asked Ava to join me. And after that fiery warning from the director, my next suggestion probably wasn't going to go over too well. "Maybe we could . . . oh, I don't know . . . hack into the station's records or something?"

Ava huffed. She looked at me as if I'd tried to insist the world was pancake flat.

Two women turned the corner ahead, walking toward us. One had a streak of purple in her black hair, and both were wearing eyeglasses.

"Hey, I'm sorry to bug you," Ava said, "but is there any chance one of you might know how to find Anna Donatelli's room?"

The one with the purple streak motioned behind her. "One-thirty-one, maybe? She's near us, right?"

The other woman shrugged. She was chewing a huge wad of gum that smelled like peppermint. She tucked it into one side of her mouth. "You're the kids," she noted.

We certainly weren't elephants. "Two of the kids, anyway," I said. "But we're the best two."

After replying with disappointingly fake laughs, the two women walked on. We moved past the kitchen and toward the dorms. "In case you forgot, this whole base is run by the US government. You can't just hack into a government computer," Ava explained. "They're encrypted."

"You hacked into Hank's computer."

"Yeah, because his password was 'ecneics,' 'science' spelled backward. Anyone could have guessed that."

Anyone but me, apparently. I'd tried about a thousand different passwords before asking for Ava's help.

The door to room 131 was open slightly when we approached. I could hear someone moving around inside. As I pressed my back against the wall to listen, Ava pushed in the door, jumped aside, and yelled, "Jack, don't go in there—that's not your room!"

"Who's that?" someone asked from inside.

Quietly impressed with my sister's trick, I stepped into the doorway. Ava pushed me forward into the room, then followed me inside. A thin man in glasses stood beside a small desk, holding a yellow plastic trash bag in one hand and a broom in the other. I'd say he was in his twenties. Old but not ancient. His nose was long, as if someone had pulled too hard on the tip. He scratched his cheek; his fingernails were long and grimy.

"Who are you?" I asked.

"I'm the Facilities Engineer."

"The what?"

"The Facilities Engineer. Or F. E. for short."

"What's that?" Ava pressed.

The F. E. adjusted his glasses. "Scientists can be a sloppy bunch. I have to clean up after them so they don't turn this place into a wreck."

"So you're a maid?"

The man glared briefly at me. "You're the smart kids?"

"I'm one of the smart kids," Ava replied. "He's just Jack."

No matter how many times she used that joke, it still stung.

"This is Dr. Donatelli's room, right?" I asked.

The F. E. shrugged. "Don't know, but this place was a disaster zone." He wiped a wet cloth across the bookshelf above the desk, then showed us the shiny residue. "There are little streaks and globs of this stuff all over the place. It smells familiar, too, but I can't quite place it."

The sticky stuff was hardly the worst of the mess. The whole room looked like it had been picked up and shaken by a giant robot. Books, clothes, and papers were scattered all over the desk, the floor, and even the bed. It didn't make any sense. "I don't get it," I said. "She's a neat freak."

"Doesn't look that way," Ava said.

I turned and whispered, "No, remember? Hank said she's super, super organized. Britney mentioned that, too."

"So?" Ava said quietly.

"So she didn't make this mess. Someone was going through her things."

"You don't need to whisper," the F. E. said. "I have very acute hearing. Typically this room is very clean, though. I hardly had to do a thing the last time I came in here."

At the desk, Ava picked up a power cord. "This goes to a laptop."

"Wow," the F. E. said, "you truly are brilliant."

Ava scowled at him. "Where's the laptop?"

The F. E. shrugged. "I haven't seen it," he said. "But enough with all the questions. I have a fun game for you two to play. Which one of you can clean this room faster?"

Ava cupped a hand to her ear and cocked her head to one

side, as if someone was speaking to her through a hidden ear-piece. Now, just so we're clear, the fake spy-phone was totally my move. I always used it when we were caught in boring conversations. But I played along. "Is that Hank?" I asked.

She paused, as if she was letting the caller finish. "Yeah," she said. "I'm sorry, sir. We'd love to help. But we've got to go."

We hurried out of the room, then stopped a few doors away. "What's the big deal with the power cord?" I asked.

"Nobody travels without them," she said. "Remember? Batteries don't last down here. It's too cold. Plus the prongs were bent, like someone ripped it out of the socket."

"So?"

"So whoever did this was in a real hurry. I think some-one stole her computer."

A trashed room. A stolen computer. Maybe our absent scientist really was in some kind of trouble.

Ava stared up at an emergency-exit sign. She slipped her backpack off her shoulders, set it down on the floor, then reached in and scoured the contents. Pulling out a small black device about the size and shape of a golf ball, she peeled something off the outside, then asked, "Can you give me a boost up to that sign?"

"What is that?"

"Boost first, questions later. And be quiet. I don't want the F. E. or the director seeing us."

Luckily, Ava is pretty light. Her feet are long but slim. As I leaned back against the wall, with my fingers clasped together below my waist, she planted one of her boots in my hands, grabbed my shoulder, and boosted herself up. Matt makes a much better stepladder, but I was trying. She fiddled briefly with the exit sign, then jumped down and landed as quietly as a cat. I shook out my fingers.

She'd pressed the black golf ball up against one side of the sign. A small glass circle in the middle, about as big as the tip of my index finger, was facing Anna's door. "Is that a lens?"

"That's my stickycam," she whispered, hurrying me away. We stopped and hid around the next corner. "I've told you about it, right?" I shook my head. She might have; sometimes my brain shuts down when my siblings talk about their ideas and inventions. "Really? Huh. Well, it's not entirely mine. Someone sent Hank a few of these little spherical video cameras. The idea was to roll them into a room to get a view of the interior before you enter." She pulled her smartphone out of her bag and scrolled through her apps. She tapped a few buttons and peeked back into the hall. "But I thought it would be cool to put some sticky material on the outside, so you could pop one of these anywhere you wanted a spy camera." She smiled and showed me her screen, which provided a decent view of Anna's doorway. "This way we'll know if our culprit tries to return the computer," she said.

"How many more of those do you have?" I asked.

She pulled three others out of her bag. Then she nodded slowly. "You're thinking we pop up a few more for surveillance?"

"Why not?"

So we did, picking spots throughout the main building. Then we headed back to Hank's room to find him sitting up in his bed, wearing socks and sandals and a hooded sweatshirt. Jazz was playing. Apparently he was deep into his work, given the music and the footwear. For a moment the tune grabbed me. I'd been listening to Hank's favorite playlists for months, hoping I might pick up a few scraps of his genius. Usually I'd try to guess the musician. This song was heavy on the drums. That meant one guy. "Art Blakey?" I asked.

Hank did not reply. He was reading through a stack of papers and writing on a yellow legal pad. The diagrams on the top sheet suggested he was analyzing entries for the Clutterbuck Prize. Ava clapped her hands a few times. He looked up, more startled than annoyed. "When did you two get here?" he asked.

Immediately we blabbered away, telling him all about the mess in Anna's room, the F. E., the missing laptop, and the stickycams. We left out the meeting with the director.

Just as we finished, Matt popped into the room. "Where

92

were you guys?" he asked, his tone soft and weak. "I was looking everywhere. You didn't even tell me—"

"Sorry, Matt, we didn't realize . . ." I looked to Ava, hoping she would help me out. Did he feel left behind?

"I agree," Hank said.

I was still trying to read Matt. "Wait," I said, turning to Hank. "What?"

He looked up from his papers and paused his music. "Oh, hello, Matthew. I was just going to say that I agree, the pieces of the puzzle do not fit. But there's little we can do at this point. I've already spoken with the director and the search and rescue team, but they all believe that Anna willingly went out alone."

"They didn't know about the missing laptop."

"I'm not sure that will be enough to convince anyone of foul play," Hank said. "The director especially. Not a very charming lady. She laughed at precisely none of my jokes."

I could not fault her for that. "What about you?" I asked. "What do you think?"

"That you need more data," Hank said. "I told you before, Anna does what she likes when she likes. For her, rules are irrelevant. Exploration, discovery—they are all that matter. So I have to say that you're going to need more than a lost laptop and some clutter to convince me—or anyone else—that she is really in danger."

# 7

# HAPPY CAMPERS

**T**HE NEXT DAY I WOKE UP WITH THE CRUD. THE WORD is kind of perfect. That's how you feel, and that's what you've got to dig out of the corners of your eyes, scrape off the edges of your lips, and pick from the rim of your nostrils. Crud. Several people had already warned us about getting dehydrated, and the inside of my mouth was as dry as sand. I chugged two glasses of water. Not even a scalding shower and some extended nose vacuuming could improve my condition, and I followed Matt and Ava into the dining room feeling like I'd been run over by Ivan the Terra Bus. The breakfast spread only made everything worse. The vat of oatmeal bubbling in the middle of the buffet had a greenish tint. The scrambled eggs were the consistency of sponge cake. I scooped some out and fire-hosed them with ketchup from a squeeze bottle.

Hank was already at the table. He glanced up at me. "You don't look that great," he said.

"I'm fine," I insisted.

Staying home at the base was not an option. Lying in bed the night before, I'd cooked up a little plan. If we could sway a few more people to believe in my theory, then we could organize a search party and go out onto the ice to find Anna ourselves. But to do that, we'd all need to pass the Happy Camper course first. So I had to go, crud or not.

With his mouth full of eggs, Matt asked, "May I test the robolegs today?"

"No, I'd rather we focus on the training."

My brother raised his eyebrows hopefully. "How about when we get back?"

"And what about that surprise you mentioned back home?" Ava asked Hank. "Didn't you talk about sending something else down here?"

"Patience, both of you, please!" Hank replied.

A rare note of frustration rang in his voice, so we finished our meal in near silence. Unfortunately, the start of the Happy Camper training program hardly improved our mood. Our education began in a gray and poorly lighted classroom. It had been two years since I was jailed in a schoolroom, and I didn't miss the experience. We sat there for hours learning all the rules and regulations of the base. Our instructors taught us how to spot signs of frostbite, identify weak points in the ice, listen for seals in the water below, tie strong knots, and use different kinds of ropes. At one point Hank tried to use his climbing rope to lasso a folding chair. He claimed he'd learned the trick from a physicist who'd lived on a Texas ranch. But he only succeeded in annoying our instructor.

Afterward, they took us through the various science labs and the Mechanical Equipment Center, where we learned about all the vehicles the researchers and rescue teams could use, including several different kinds of snowmobiles, a machine called a PistenBully, which had the tracked wheels of an army tank, and a big, beautiful beast that resembled a miniaturized, luxury version of Ivan the Terra Bus. Its knobby tires were as tall as my shoulders. The blue paint was so clean, it gleamed, and "Rambler" was painted on the door in white cursive script. I tried to climb up into the driver's seat, but one of our instructors grabbed me before I even got close. Ava and Matt listened as the man told me that the Rambler was the director's prized possession. The vehicle could carry ten passengers, plow through a wall, and outrace a snowmobile. And he warned us that she'd probably find out if we even looked at it too long, let alone jumped into the driver's seat.

The Rambler would have been much nicer than the rumbling vehicle we rode across the ice shelf. I'll spare you the details of the journey, such as how we learned to use the major landmarks, like the cloud-belching volcano, to figure out our location in the middle of all that ice. Some of it was interesting. Honestly. But I'm jumping to the really good part.

We learned how to build snow forts.

And not just any snow forts, but some of the biggest, strongest, and warmest frozen houses you've ever seen. We constructed small ones, too, which were just large enough to lie down inside of without touching the walls. But my favorite was the shelter that would be our home for the night.

First we threw all our gear into a giant pile. Next we started shoveling snow on top of our equipment. That's right. We buried our most important possessions. Following the lead of our instructor, a flat-nosed, long-haired Italian man named Angelo, Matt worked like a machine, hurling one heavy shovelful of snow after another onto the growing mound. Occasionally he'd glance at Hank, but his idol was too busy talking to Angelo to notice his hard work. Ava and me? We tried to help. A little, anyway.

When Angelo said the mound was large enough, we packed down the snow, then began digging a tunnel to reach the equipment from below. Next we carefully pulled the gear through the tunnel until it was all outside. This left a huge, snow-covered space where our stuff had been. Finally, we dug out the inner portion a little more, so you could actually stand up in the middle of the shelter.

Once we were all inside, we wolfed down a few chocolate bars. Did I forget to mention that candy was pretty much one of the major food groups down at the South Pole? It's true. Everyone here actually suggests bringing at least three candy bars with you whenever you're going outside because you burn calories so quickly. As we ate, Angelo reminded us to drink as much as we could, too. Even though we were surrounded by snow, Antarctica was as dry as the desert, so he wanted to make sure we stayed hydrated. Then he set a metal stove in the middle of the floor. With a few quick jabs he punched a soccer-ball-size hole right through a wall, opening a kind of window to the outside. I thought he was angry. I slid over to Ava and asked, "Did we do something wrong?"

Angelo heard me and laughed. "This is just to let the shelter breathe. You should not punch the ceiling, though, okay?"

"How about the ice?" I patted the frozen floor of our shelter. "You're sure this is solid?"

"Very," Angelo said. "You would need a fairly big drill to get through to the water here. In other places the ice is thinner. There you might see seals popping up through small holes to breathe. You learned about those seal holes in class, right?" We nodded. "And they warned you about trapdoors, yes?"

Ava scooted forward to answer. "When the seal holes

freeze over, a thin layer of ice forms. You can't see it sometimes."

"That is exactly why we come out onto the ice!" Angelo said. "You cannot learn everything in the classroom." He smacked his lips. "Indoors you cannot feel the dryness of the air or spot a potential pitfall. We will show you what these dangers are like in the real world, because you do not want to step on a trapdoor."

Matt tapped Ava's shoulder. "You should send Shelly down through one of those," he suggested.

"She's not ready," Ava said.

Later, I heard the whine of an engine. Hank and Matt were talking with Angelo about the physics of our fort, and why an ice-encrusted snow house could be so delightfully warm. Ava was fiddling with Fred; the defunct smartphone she now used to control him was resting on her knee.

As the engine noise grew louder, everyone but Ava looked up.

"Who's that?" Hank asked.

Angelo crawled to the fort's entrance, reached out, and pushed aside the flap he'd placed there to block the wind. A snowmobile was speeding toward us in a swirl of white. Angelo flopped back to his seat. "This is my ride," he said. "I must return to the base. There is a contest tonight."

"Trivia?" Matt asked.

"No, no," Angelo said. "We had a trivia contest once, but a question about the origin of the universe sparked an argument, which turned into a fistfight. Luckily no one was hurt because cosmologists don't throw very good punches. But there are no more trivia contests down here. Now we sing. Tonight is our weekly karaoke contest."

"So you're leaving us out here all alone for a karaoke contest?" Ava asked.

"Of course not!" Angelo reached out and patted her on the shoulder, laughing. "Otherwise you would all be Popsicles by morning." The engine outside stopped. Angelo leaned forward and pushed open the flap again. A square-shaped man climbed off the snowmobile; Angelo gathered his things in an excited rush. "I am taking the snowmobile and my friend is staying here. He will take good care of you. If you have trouble sleeping, you should ask him to sing. He has the voice of an angel. He should really be going back for the contest, to tell you the truth, but he refuses to compete. Anyway, I will see you back at the base soon. Remember, keep drinking water, and eat your candy."

I laughed. Had an adult ever said that to a kid before?

A blast of frigid air whipped through the tiny doorway as Angelo crawled out. A moment later his replacement wriggled inside. He removed his frosted goggles, then pulled off his icicle-encrusted helmet and a red woolen hat.

Our new instructor was short and thick. Gray stubble was sprouting all around his very round head, and his eyebrows looked thick enough to braid. He rocked his chin back and forth, revealing jaw muscles I didn't know existed. Then he dropped heavily to a seat on our icy floor and let out a sigh so powerful, I could feel his breath on my cheeks. Even with my crud-packed nose I could tell that it reeked of sausage. Apple sausage. How in the world could someone who blew such pungent mouth wind have the voice of an angel?

A normal person would have said hello. Our new friend just nodded. Were we supposed to introduce ourselves? Ask him for his name? Thank him for coming all the way out here to make sure we didn't turn into Popsicles? I had no idea, and a glance around our frozen room confirmed that the geniuses were just as confused.

The man sneered at Fred, shook his head, and remarked in a thick accent, "In America, even children have drones now, eh?" Before anyone could reply, he sneezed and wiped his nose on his sleeve. He needed a few minutes with the vacuum. But there was no way I was going to let him shove that precious device up one of his cavernous nostrils.

He lit the small metal stove in the center of the floor and leaned back. A blue and orange flame flickered and waved. He looked at me. "And now?" he asked.

Luckily, I'd been listening in all those survival classes. "Snow, right?"

"Yes! Very good," he said.

I piled a few handfuls of snow into our small metal pot, then placed it atop the stove's blue flame.

"Your accent is Russian, right?" Ava asked.

"Yes, Russian," our new instructor said. "I am Evgeny Evgenovich Levokin."

Levokin? This was the guy who had joined Anna on previous expeditions. The one Britney had suggested as a possible suspect. And now we were stuck with him in a frozen hut, miles from anyone or anywhere. I'd be lying if I said I wasn't a little excited.

"Eugene Junior," Ava said.

"What?" I asked.

"In Russian his middle name means 'son of Eugene.' It's called a patronymic."

"Very nice," Levokin said. "You speak Russian?"

"No, I only read it," Ava said. "Pushkin, mostly."

Next she was going to mention that she also read French, Italian, and Spanish. I had to stop her before it got ugly. "We have some questions for you," I said.

"About Pushkin?"

"No," Matt added. "About Anna Donatelli. Right, Jack?"

Levokin cursed. Or at least I think he cursed. He spat

out a bunch of Russian words I didn't understand. "That minx stole my skin," he said at last.

"Your skin?" Matt asked.

"My life's work," he said. "The greatest wet suit ever designed. It is like a new layer of skin for the diver. Normal wet suits keep divers warm for only twenty minutes. Mine protects you for hours."

Ava sat forward. "Hours?"

"Hours! It is beautiful, my wet suit, and the one I lent to Anna was the only prototype." With a long wooden spoon he stirred the quickly melting snow. Something was glimmering at the corner of his eyes. Was our suspect actually getting teary?

"Well, that is disheartening, but we're all looking forward to seeing your other invention in action at the demonstration on Sunday," Hank said.

Deep creases formed on Levokin's forehead. "My other invention?"

"For the Clutterbuck Prize," Matt said.

"The what?"

"You know, the award for the inventor who can come up with a more efficient way to make drinking water out of saltwater."

"Clutterbuck . . . this is the man with the socks?"

"That's right."

103

"Yes, I love this man!" He lifted up the legs of his pants and pulled at the top of his socks. "I have not changed these in fourteen days." With effort he pulled off one of his boots. "Wonderful socks. Go ahead, smell. Please."

The others declined, but I braved a gentle whiff. I caught very faint hints of toe cheese, and maybe salami, but nothing too potent. "Not bad," I said.

"Yes, I admire this Clutterbuck," Levokin said. "But I am not trying to win his prize. Must be mistake."

"How odd," Hank said.

While Matt leaned forward to smell our new instructor's socks, I watched Levokin closely. His face was relaxed. He wasn't avoiding anyone's gaze. Was he really telling the truth? Or was it all part of a grand lie? Matt coughed. Levokin was still smiling. "Back to our missing scientist," I said. "Do you know where she is, Mr. Levokin?"

"No," he answered.

"Could you guess?" Ava asked.

"I will tell you what I know," he said. "But first we have hot chocolate."

Levokin removed a few square white packets from our kit of rations. He flicked his finger against the side of one, shook it, and repeated the process with the others. Slowly he began to talk. "I meet Dr. Donatelli for first time last year. I had written some papers on wet-suit design, using the seal as inspiration." He shivered. "I don't like these creatures. Very slimy. But very good at staying warm underwater. Beautiful adaptation. I had ideas for copying seals to make better wet suit. She convinces me to make her a prototype and let her test it. I agree. I make wet suit, come all the way down here to South Pole. We go to our first camp. Anna, myself, two engineers from McMurdo. Good men. A little smelly, but strong. On first day, she dives for three hours at a time in this frigid sea."

"And?" Matt asked. "What did she find?"

"What did she find?" he roared. "Who cares what she finds? She dove for three hours! This was impossible before my wet suit." The snow in the pot was fully melted, the water boiling. He lined up five tin cups and sprinkled chocolate powder into each. Then he filled the mugs halfway with steaming water and passed them around. "This Clutterbuck Prize," he said. "Why can't you just melt snow, like this?"

I studied his face. Did he really not know? Or was he hiding something?

"We use too much water as it is," Hank explained. "If we melted snow, there wouldn't be any left on Ross Island. Plus, it would take too much energy. The goal is to find a more efficient and less expensive method. Now, you were talking about your expedition with Anna . . ."

"Yes. Okay. So after few days," he said, holding a

steaming cup just below his chin, "she looks in her notebook at her little map, and she tells us we are going to move on. This next place was same story. Lots of looking. Lots of Anna swimming. No big findings. No new creatures to make Dr. Golding jealous. Then one day we wake up, no Anna. Snowmobile is missing, too, but tracks are buried from the snow and wind, so we don't know where she has gone. And no wet suit!" He slammed down his fist.

Startled, I spilled some of my hot chocolate over the rim. "That was Tuesday?" I asked.

"No, I'm talking about first time she disappeared. Tuesday night was second time."

"Wait," Hank said. "Back up again. Where'd she go with your wet suit the first time?"

"And what kind of creatures was she looking for?" Matt asked.

The Russian held up a finger. The knuckles were like small, dented golf balls. "Ah, these things she does not tell us! So, last week. We had been out on ice for long time already. Then, Thursday morning—"

"A week ago today," I said.

"Yes? A week ago. Why is this so hard? So. Thursday morning, she takes snowmobile and leaves us note. She promises she will be back in two days. Food in fridge, plenty of water, enough to survive. Sure. But this was not allowed! This leaving us alone and disappearing was not what we agreed. So we radio the base."

"You sold her out," I said.

"What does this mean? I didn't sell anyone."

"No, I mean, you told on her. You got her into trouble."

"She abandoned us in small hut on ice sheet! These other men, they smell like woolly mammoths." He pinched his nose. "Dead woolly mammoths. We could not stay there two more days."

Matt slurped some of his hot chocolate.

"Phobos, Matthew," Hank said. Then he asked Levokin, "So what happened when you got back to McMurdo?"

Levokin sneezed again. He still wasn't getting a turn with my vacuum. "Everything must be approved here, yes? Well, when we are picked up, we discover that Anna was only approved to be in the field for five days. We had already stayed ten days. She was in very deep trouble. There was talk of sending her home on the next plane. The director . . . you have met her?" Hank nodded. I elbowed Ava. "She is not very warm. Cold and brutal as Herbie storm. She was mad. Very. Then Anna comes back to McMurdo on Monday morning with smile as bright as star. The director says she will be sent home, but Anna does not care."

"Why not?" I asked.

Hank edged closer to the Russian. "She found a new species, right? New sea creatures?"

Levokin's enormous eyebrows rose twice in silent confirmation.

"That was Monday?" I asked.

He rocked his head back and forth, then whistled briefly. "Monday. Yes. I am certain. She returns with my wet suit. The next night, Tuesday, I am sitting in my room, playing violin, very nice tune, very relaxing, when the crazy woman bursts through the door and starts to search my bags and my desk. 'Where are they?' she cries. 'Where are my babies?'"

Matt scooted forward on his knees. "The creatures?"

"Yes, yes. I tell her I don't have them, but it takes some time for her to believe me. Finally, she apologizes. She says someone has stolen her creatures, her computer, more. Then later that night she disappears again with my wet suit."

Ava looked at me, half smiling. She had been right about the laptop.

"You didn't lock it up?"

Levokin shrugged. "I didn't think the thief would steal it twice."

In my head I was trying to picture it all. Monday Anna had returned triumphant. Britney had mentioned that. Then on Tuesday she was panicking. What happened in between?

Clearly someone had stolen her work. Maybe destroyed it. And the director was threatening to send her home. So she ran off with Levokin's wet suit to look for more samples. All of that I understood. But why didn't she leave Hank a message? Or tell someone else? Why did she have to be all sneaky about the whole thing?

"She must've gone back to the same site," Hank said. "The place where she found the creatures when she left you at the camp. Do you have any idea where that might be?"

"This I hope you could tell to me," Levokin said. "She didn't send you note? Call you? Maybe write e-mail?"

A long pause followed. The interior of our snow fort became uncomfortably quiet. Even the wind decided to stop, as if it were waiting for an answer.

Then I noticed that the geniuses were staring at me.

Levokin joined them. "Why are we looking at this one?" he asked.

Hank squinted. He lowered his voice. "Jack?"

"Jack," Matt added, "you have been checking Hank's e-mail, right?"

# 8

# MYSTERIOUS MESSAGE

**S**O, YEAH. I FORGOT. BUT, HONESTLY, CAN YOU BLAME me? A lot had been happening. Sure, checking Hank's e-mail is supposed to be my job, and the geniuses were really quick to remind me of that fact, but it's not like anyone else remembered, either. Was it really all my fault?

The worst part was that we couldn't check it right away. We hadn't been allowed to bring phones or computers, and there isn't exactly Wi-Fi out on the ice shelf, anyway. So we suffered through a mostly sleepless night. At one point Levokin started singing, and while his voice was unusually beautiful, it didn't hustle me on my way to dreamland. Instead, it kept me awake.

In the morning, we quickly packed our gear. A Pisten-Bully picked us up, and although it was toasty warm in the back, I swear the old lady with the walker on the first floor of our apartment building could have outraced the machine.

When we finally got back to the base, we dashed to Hank's room. Matt tripped at one point, and I didn't even laugh. I was too anxious. Sure enough, there was a note from Anna waiting in Hank's inbox, but it wasn't quite as revealing as we'd hoped. We each read it four or five times before anyone said anything. Her message was short:

> *Sadly, I won't be able to greet you. Some unpleasant developments. Left you a map to my location, safely tucked away with my first love. If I'm not back soon, please come find me.*

Hank started drumming his long fingers on his chin.

Ava turned to him. "So, how do we find this map? What does she mean by her first love? Was that you?"

"What? First love? No! We never . . . I mean, there were fleeting moments . . . maybe during the cocktail hour at that biology conference in Paris, but I don't recall that particular . . . emotion ever surfacing . . ."

"Is it possible?"

"No."

"So she definitely wasn't your girlfriend?" Ava asked. "Like Min isn't your girlfriend?"

"No! No now, and no again tomorrow, okay?"

There was a knock at the door. Someone we hadn't met

111

leaned through: a woman with short graying hair and a sun-wrinkled face. "Dr. Witherspoon? You're supposed to be at the Clutterbuck Prize meeting."

"Right, right. When does it start?"

"Eleven minutes ago. As you know, several of the contestants will be videoconferencing in, since they could not make the trip, but a few others just arrived this morning. One of our own engineers is competing as well."

"Yes, the Australian fellow," Hank said. He glanced down at his watch. "We'll have to talk about this later, guys."

"But Anna's out there all alone," I protested.

Hank turned to our visitor. "Could you give us thirty seconds? I'll be right along." The door closed. He gestured at the computer screen. "She's out there by choice, Jack! The e-mail makes that clear."

"Yes, but someone's definitely after her," I said. "Why else would she be so sneaky? Why would she hide the map?"

"She knows what she's doing," Hank insisted. "And we'll find her. We'll find a way. We can talk about everything when I get out of this meeting."

"But you keep saying—"

"I promise. Okay? Later. We'll come up with a plan later."

The door closed behind him, then opened again. "I forgot," he said. "You're in my room. All three of you, out."

We followed orders, and out in the hall Ava was already on the move. "Let's get our coats," she said.

"Why?" I asked.

"Maybe she's like me. Her first love, I mean."

The image of a kid from our old neighborhood popped into my mind. He was tall and skinny, and his glasses were square and small. He could recite pi to a hundred decimal places, and Ava thought he was dreamy. "What does Stephen Famigletti have to do with anything?" I asked.

"Ew, gross," she said. "I'm not talking about him."

Matt laughed. "Her first love was science, you Neanderthal."

"Before engineering won my heart."

"Oh, right. So then you're thinking . . ."

Ava gave me her I'll-slow-it-down-just-this-once look—a dramatically prolonged roll of the eyes. "If her first love was science, and she hid the map with her first love, then the logical place to look would be . . ."

I needed way too long to figure it out. She started to answer for me, but I shushed her. "The science lab?"

"See?" she said, patting me on the back. "You're not completely hopeless."

The Albert P. Crary Science and Engineering Center was a short, cold walk down a hard dirt road. Matt, Ava, and I grabbed our Big Reds from our room and braved the bright

113

blue night. Our breath kicked out thick clouds as we hurried along the road to the center's three connected buildings, or pods. I was still fighting my cold, and wrapped my arms around my chest to keep away the chill. From our tour during the Happy Camper classes, we knew the first and largest of the pods housed labs, offices, and special equipment, and I pushed inside ahead of the others.

"What happened to 'ladies first'?" Ava asked.

"You're not a lady. You're my sister."

We hurried down an enclosed hallway to reach the second pod, where a different set of scientists had their labs, and then descended another long, narrow hallway to reach the third and final building. That's where they kept the aquatic life, and where Anna would have her work space. At McMurdo they called it the aquarium. But to me an aquarium is a dark, musty space filled with screaming kids and parents who want to look at the fish, which don't care at all about the visiting humans unless one of us is swimming past with food. This place was more like a workshop. It housed several small labs, an electronics shop, and a large space lined with workbenches, computer stations, and tanks that held all sorts of wonderful, exotic, aquatic creatures.

The polished cement floor was stained dark in places. The air had a slightly metallic taste. A tall man in a blue lab coat was picking apart some kind of filter in the middle of the room. I recognized him. But I couldn't remember where I'd seen him before. He caught me staring and grunted.

I turned away. "So, where do we start?"

"Maybe we just look around," Ava suggested.

"Back already? How was Happy Camper?" Danno had snuck up behind us like some kind of oversize Australian ninja.

"You scared me," Ava said.

"Not me," I lied.

"Pretty neat place, right?" Danno said. "There are organisms in here that don't exist anywhere else in the world. You ever seen one of these?" he asked, leading us over to a large rectangular aquarium. Reddish creatures that looked like starfish mixed with alien DNA crawled across the stones on the bottom of the tank.

A laminated form was attached to the base of the aquarium. Matt pointed to the name in block letters. "This is Dr. Golding's workbench?" he asked.

"Guess so, mate," Danno said. "Every scientist down here gets assigned their own work space. Kind of like how you're given a desk in school."

"We don't go to school," Ava noted.

"Is Golding here?" Matt asked.

"No, he's out in the field," Danno said. "He should be back soon enough, though. He wouldn't miss the karaoke competition Saturday night."

"Didn't you just have a contest?" I asked.

"Yes, but Saturday night is the big one. The grand championship. He's the favorite to win again this year."

"You sure do love your karaoke down here," Ava noted.

"Where's Anna's workstation?" Matt asked.

He nodded to the man in the blue lab coat. "Walter's the one who assigns everyone their lab bench. He'd know, but he's as prickly as a cactus, so I'm sure not going to ask him." Danno pointed to a small workbench against the farthest wall. "I think I saw her name on that one, though."

We wandered over. Danno was right about the name, but the table was empty except for a square tank the size of several milk cartons. "There's nothing in here," I said.

Matt stood next to me and swept a finger across the aluminum surface, clearing a path through a thin layer of dust. "No one has worked here for a while."

The radio clipped to Danno's belt buzzed. "What are you looking for, anyway?"

Behind us, the doors to the lab opened. A few researchers walked through, talking and smiling. One of them waved to Danno. "How's the luck? You feeling like a Clutterbuck winner?"

116

"I believe they're known as Clutterbuckians," one of the others said.

That definitely wasn't true.

"Just don't forget us when you pocket that million, okay?" said the first man.

"Never, Mark," Danno said. "I'll never forget I've stood on the shoulders of donkeys."

The three researchers laughed.

Danno's radio started buzzing again. A muffled voice was saying something about the Clutterbuck meeting. Finally he yanked the radio off his belt and held it to the side of his face. "Sorry! I'll be there in a minute," he said. Then he turned back to us and smiled. "Let me know if you need help with anything."

Matt pulled up a stool and leaned against the dust-covered table. "She had to work somewhere, right? So if not here, then where?" He lifted his chin toward the man in the blue lab coat. "Should we ask him?"

Ava crossed her arms on her chest. "I'm not doing it."

"Me, neither," Matt said.

And so the job was mine. I plastered on my most charming smile, walked over to Walter, and introduced myself.

Walter practically barked at me. "What do you want?"

"We're hoping to find out where Dr. Donatelli worked."

Walter started to point to the dusty table. "No, I don't mean her official space. I'm talking about where she really worked."

Walter set down his wrench. He leaned over and looked back at Matt and Ava. Then he breathed in slowly through his nose, crossed his hairy forearms on his wide chest, and stared at me through half-closed eyes. "I might know something."

"You might know something?"

Walter nodded. "I might."

Our eyes locked in a deadly serious stare. Something told me he'd give me the information if I gave him something in return. But what did he want? Money? A nose vacuum? Maybe a pair of self-drying boxers? We studied each other in silence, and then I remembered where I'd seen him before. At dinner the first night he was sitting at the table next to us. He was the one who'd spat out his coffee.

"And I might have something that would interest you."

"What's that?"

"Some very rare and delicious civet coffee beans."

His hardened frown faded. He bit his lower lip. "Really? Civet beans? Show me."

I zipped up my Big Red, told my siblings I'd be right back, and raced to the room to fetch the coffee beans. When I returned, Matt and Ava were perched on stools across from Walter. They were both trying not to smile. I put the bag of beans down in front of Walter. He inhaled the scent of the contents with his eyes closed.

"What? Why are you two smiling?"

"Tell you later," Ava said.

Walter removed a tarnished silver key from a drawer and slid it across the desk to me. "The basketball court. The equipment closet on the left side, as you enter. I helped her set up a work space in there because she wanted privacy, and, well, we don't get too many basketball junkies down here at the Pole. I swore I wouldn't tell anyone," he added, "but I'm desperate for good coffee."

Matt and Ava gave in to their laughter. I ignored them. "Thank you, Walter. We appreciate it."

As we hurried out of the pod, I asked, "What was that all about?"

They giggled again. "Do you know where civet beans come from?"

I'd planned to read about them but there was never any time. "No. Why?"

"You go," Ava said to Matt.

He could barely get out the words. "The civet is a catlike mammal that lives in Southeast Asia, only it looks more like a rodent."

"So?"

119

"So, civet coffee is made of beans that the civet has eaten and partially digested and then—"

Ava couldn't resist. "They're poop beans!"

I closed my eyes. This was horribly disappointing and disgusting news, but I tried to pretend I didn't care. At least now I understood why Jen, our hostess on Clutterbuck's jet, was smiling so strangely when she gave me the gift. "Well," I said, "those critter droppings make delicious coffee."

Suddenly I didn't feel so bad about giving them away.

At the exit, we were zipping up our coats when Britney pushed through the doors. She stomped her boots and pulled down her hood. Her cheeks were red from the cold. She tilted her head and squinted at me. "What are you kids doing down here in the labs?"

"Nothing?" Matt replied, suddenly blushing.

I shut my eyes for a second. My brother would make a horrible spy. "We were just looking around," I said.

Britney reached forward to zip up Ava's Big Red, which was open at the top. My sister recoiled and did it herself. "Does Hank know you're out here?" Britney asked.

"We don't have to tell him everywhere we go," Ava snapped.

"Well, you shouldn't be roaming around," Britney replied.

"We know," Matt said, "but we were—"

"The director is looking for any reason to kick you three

out of here early," Britney added. "Don't give her one, okay?"

Matt answered before I could reply. "Understood," he said.

"And remember, it's cold out there." She glanced at Ava's jacket again. "They gave you these jackets for a reason."

As Britney continued on her way, Ava muttered something about how we weren't little kids. Matt started to reply, then wisely kept quiet, and we hurried back to the main building. The basketball court was empty when we arrived. The air smelled dusty. We unlocked the former equipment closet, flicked on the light, stepped inside, and closed the door. I sneezed twice into the elbow of my Big Red. The room was barely big enough for the three of us. While Matt and I searched for the map, Ava sorted through the electronic parts and pieces that were neatly arranged on the tabletop crowded into the closet.

There was barely a sheet of paper in the whole closet, let alone a map. "I don't see it," I said.

"Me neither," Matt said.

Ava held up a small box attached to a neoprene band. She slipped the band around her head. A lens the size of a half-dollar was facing out of the little box.

"That doesn't look like a map," I said.

"It's a headcam," she said. "I bet Anna used this when she was diving."

121

With her fingernails she popped open the camera's waterproof case. She removed a small black plastic square the size of a postage stamp, flicked on the desk lamp, and held the square under the light. A second later she beamed as brightly as a treasure hunter who had just discovered a rare diamond.

"Is that a memory card?" I asked.

"Well, it's not a donut," Ava said.

That was unnecessary; I was proud of my guess.

She scraped off a whitish brown crust from the black square and touched some of it to her tongue. "A little salt corrosion, but it should still work. Matt, what do you think it has on here?" she asked.

He folded his arms across his chest and drummed his fingers on his chin, trying to look like Hank. "Video, obviously. But there's a good chance it has geotags."

"In English, please," I said.

Ava held up the tiny square. "A geotag is a record of where this device has been and at what time. So if Anna used this camera on her last trip, then this little card might tell us where she went when she snuck away from Levokin, and if we know that . . ."

I didn't need help finishing her sentence. "Then we don't need the map, after all."

# 9

# GENIUS IS OVERRATED

TYPICALLY I LOVE IT WHEN THE GENIUSES ARE WRONG. Really. I float on a cloud of happy unicorn dust for days. This time? Not so much. The memory card only stored video, not a neat and tidy record of Anna Donatelli's recent travels. It contained hours of footage of Anna swimming through the strange world between the ice shelf and the seafloor, which was scattered with starfish and crabs. Watching the video in our room was mesmerizing. I felt as if I was kicking through that eerie blue world myself, only without the heart-stopping cold. But the video didn't give us answers. Instead, it sparked about a thousand more questions, and one scene proved especially strange.

When Hank came into our room after his meeting, he was drawn in immediately. On the video, little white globs appeared to be floating up from the seafloor toward the ice surface. Hank pointed to a spot on the screen, jabbing it with his index finger. Ava winced; she was constantly reminding him that not all laptops were touch-sensitive. "What's that?" he asked.

"That's what we're trying to figure out," Matt said.

"It's not plankton," Hank decided. "Plankton would drift. This material is floating straight up."

Matt nodded. "Maybe it's less dense than the surrounding water."

"You all understand density, don't you?" Hank asked. He'd said "you all," but he was looking directly at me. I did understand the basic idea, and I started to say as much, but he didn't listen. "Think of an ice cube. When you drop an ice cube into a glass of water, what happens?"

They waited for me to answer. All three of them. I rolled my eyes. "It floats to the top," I said.

"Right! Exactly. Because frozen water has a lower density than liquid water. That basically means it has fewer particles, or molecules, of water packed into the same space. Something with higher density has more particles packed into the same space."

"So are those ice cubes?" I asked.

Everyone went silent.

"No . . ." Matt answered. His response was slow and hesitant. Not definitive. He glanced at Hank. "Right?"

Again they were quiet. I couldn't tell if my question was

brilliant or completely idiotic. "How is this going to help us find Anna?" I asked.

Both Ava and Matt looked to Hank.

"Well," he said, "if we study the surroundings closely, the depth of the water, maybe even the thickness of the ice, we might be able to narrow down the possible locations."

"So the map would be easier," I pointed out.

"Yeah," Ava said, "but we don't know where it is, remember?"

"Britney might be able to help," Matt suggested. "She knows this seascape better than we do. Maybe she'd recognize the spot."

As Hank edged his finger back toward the screen, Ava held her own hand close, ready to slap Hank's pointer away. Looking at the three of them, I realized it was going to be a long night. I could've poured a cold bowl of soup onto Hank's head and he wouldn't have turned away from that screen. But I didn't test that theory. In part because I didn't have any soup.

"I'll go get Britney," I offered. "Any idea where I'd find her at this hour?"

"This time the other night she was at the gym," Matt said.

Ava laughed. "You would know that."

125

Ignoring her, Matt said to me, "I'll go with you."

Sure enough, our blue-eyed friend was jogging on one of the dozen treadmills in McMurdo's gymnasium. A huge hardcover book was propped open on the control panel in front of her. In one corner of the gym a man was lifting large weights, but otherwise the room was empty. The man was breathing dramatically, and I could only see the back of his gray buzz cut. Before Britney spotted us, Matt walked over to a set of free weights and lifted one a few times.

"Are you serious?" I asked.

"What? I'm just working out."

I was all set to dare him to lift something impossibly heavy when Britney called us over. Her treadmill slowed to a walking pace.

"What're you reading?" I asked, raising my voice above the low whine of the machine.

"Asimov," she said. "One of the greats. There's a decent selection of science fiction in the library, if you're interested. What's up? Here to exercise?"

Matt stammered. I almost felt bad for him.

"The geniuses need you," I said.

"The geniuses?"

I pointed my thumb at Matt and clarified, "My brother, Ava, Hank."

"Oh," she said. Then she leaned forward over the

treadmill. "You know, Jack, genius is overrated. All humans have large and beautiful brains. You just have to work yours, like a muscle."

The weight lifter grunted. What Britney said meant something. I know. But the man's roars were comical. Quietly we all laughed.

"Who is that?" Matt asked, half whispering.

"I told you about him already," she said. "That's Victor Valenza."

Right: the diver we'd seen in the cafeteria. This time his ears looked even. "One of our suspects," I added.

Matt flicked me on the shoulder. "Should we talk to him? You know, to gather more data, like Hank said?"

I remembered my brother's saddened, rejected face after Ava and I had gone sleuthing without him. "That's a good idea," I said. "Let's do it."

"You said the others need me, right? I'm happy to help," Britney said. "Would one of you mind filling me in on the walk back to your room?"

Matt glanced between Britney and the grunting diver. My brother's face was as easy to read as a picture book: detective work had suddenly become less interesting. "Why don't you take Britney, Matt? You'll be better at explaining everything. I'll talk to Mr. Valenza here."

Britney placed her hand on Matt's elbow and led him

toward the door. "He calls you Matt," she noted. "I really think Matthew suits you, though. Much more mature. Now, tell me, what have you geniuses been up to?"

I thought my brother was going to faint, but talking science always eased his nerves, and he was describing the video in detail before they'd walked three steps. Meanwhile, I sauntered over to the rack of dumbbells and grabbed the one that Matt had just hoisted with ease.

"That's too big for you," Valenza grumbled from a few steps away.

I tried to lift it anyway. It didn't move. Matt was stronger than I'd thought. "Is there extra gravity down here?"

"You shouldn't lift weights until you're at least fourteen." He squinted, focusing on my straw-thin arms. "Then again, maybe you should start now . . ."

"Thanks," I said, extending my hand. "I'm Jack."

He crushed my puny fingers in a death grip. "Yes, I know."

"You are Victor Valenza, the greatest ice diver the South Pole has ever known." I paused, allowing him to inflate with pride. Then I struck with my verbal pin. "Before Anna Donatelli came along."

Again I waited. I watched his face for signs of rising rage. Reddening eyes. A muscle popping in his jaw. Clenched fists. Yet he didn't betray a spark of anger.

128

"You mistake me for a ukulele, my skinny friend."

"What?"

"The ukulele is perhaps the easiest string instrument to play. I'm more of a mandolin. Infinitely more complex." He cracked his knuckles. "You are trying to play me, aren't you? My question is, why? I think we'd save ourselves some time if you just told me."

So I already knew he was stronger than me. Now I knew that he was craftier, too. "Okay, fine. I'm wondering if you had anything to do with Anna Donatelli's disappearance."

"Why would I . . . Oh!" He snapped his fingers. The sound was so loud, my ears practically popped. "You think I'm jealous about my diving records?"

"She did break them all."

"Yes, but that would be no reason to exile her to a frozen wilderness. Besides, those records mean nothing." His gaze darted to the floor. That little movement meant everything.

"Really? Nothing?"

Valenza wagged one of his fingers at me. "You're good. Very good. Okay. Fine. I may have sent a note or two to the director, protesting her use of Levokin's wet suit. But you have to understand, it's not fair. That equipment gives her an enormous advantage. It would be like someone driving a car in a footrace."

"You sound jealous to me."

129

"Look," he said, "I understand what you're doing. I appreciate your concern, but I didn't have anything to do with her disappearance. I've barely even spoken to the woman. If you want to find out more about Donatelli, don't talk to me. Talk to Sophie."

"Sophie?"

"One of the chefs," he said. "Sometimes I sneak into the kitchen at night"—he patted his belly—"for extra sustenance. Many times I saw them talking quietly together there." Victor Valenza lifted his nose, inhaled, and smiled rapturously. "You should go if you want to find Sophie. It smells like she's in the kitchen now."

"You can smell her?"

"No, not her. The bread. Follow the baking bread, my friend."

Instead of risking another handshake, I thanked the burly diver with a wave and hurried to the cafeteria. Inside, Mr. Frosty was gurgling. A light above his handle blinked red; he was either broken or empty. I pushed through the swinging metal doors to the kitchen. Warm, delicious air swept past my face. Suddenly I was hungrier than a starved lion. The room was divided into four aisles lined with counters, ovens, tall steel freezers and fridges, and metal cabinets. The aroma of the freshly baked bread only grew stronger inside. At first the room was silent except for the low hum of the refrigerating units. Then something cracked and splattered in the next aisle. A woman muttered in a foreign language. French, I guessed. I tiptoed over and peered around a giant steel freezer.

A female chef was cleaning a few broken eggs off the floor. Her black hair was buzzed on the sides and back, longish on top. She had green eyes and little silver hoops in her eyebrows. The doors of a large steel fridge hung open as she cleaned the shells and yolk off the floor. Once she finished, she carefully removed a large, cube-shaped plastic container from the fridge and set it down on the counter. She leaned over the container, looking into it, and started talking to whatever was inside. Thankfully, even though she cursed in a foreign language, she spoke to her food in English. "Hello, little babies. Are you okay? Did that scare you? It's okay, it's okay, my little friends. Sophie will take care of you. Sophie will change your water."

Next she took a large slotted spoon and began scooping what looked like miniature icicles out of the water. She slid them off the spoon onto a paper towel, folded over the edges, and patted them briefly. Then she removed a large, half-filled Mason jar from underneath the steel counter, unscrewed the top, and funneled the icicles inside. Five or six times she repeated the process, harvesting the ice, rolling it around on a towel, then dumping it into the jar. Then she

131

scribbled something on the lid with a Sharpie and peered back down into the plastic container. "Okay," she said, "is that better? I'll get you some new water."

Now she reached into the fridge, removed another jar, and poured its contents into the container. Was this some kind of recipe? And if so, why was she talking to her ingredients? "There," she said, "there's some nice cold saltwater for you. Does that feel better? I'm so glad I came to check on you. Your mommy would not be happy if I neglected her little babies."

Mommy? What in the name of Mr. Frosty was going on? The bottom of the world was getting stranger by the second, and I forgot to hide my confusion. I don't know if I grunted or laughed, but Sophie spun around and glared at me from under those pierced eyebrows.

I stood up and faced the French chef. "Who's Mommy?"

"Zut."

"English, please."

"Zut, zut, zut," she said.

There was nothing scientific about what happened next. I simply followed my instincts. "Look," I said. "We're your friends. Anna's friends. Hank and Ava and I and my brother, Matt." I stopped to correct myself; no sense missing an opportunity. "Sorry, he prefers Matthew. But, anyway, we're here to help Anna, and we need to find her to make sure she's safe."

132

After a moment she replied, "You are truly her friends?"

"Yes. Honestly."

Sophie stepped away, and I moved forward to look into the plastic container. Down at the bottom, four or five yellowish creatures about the size of my hand moved around slowly. They weren't starfish, exactly. Or octopi. But they certainly weren't fish. To be honest, they looked like something that might come flying out the nose of a sneezing giant. And they were definitely alive. They were crawling over one another, creeping around, squelching along the bottom. I shivered. I had no doubt that the little monsters were going to have a starring role in my next nightmare. "What are those things?" I asked. "More important, do you have any chocolate ice cream? I think Mr. Frosty is broken."

A timer dinged in the distance. Sophie laughed, then lay one arm across her apron, propped the elbow of her other arm on her wrist, dropped her forehead to her hand, and shook her head. "Okay, okay. I will tell you what I know. First I must get my baguettes. *Allons-y.*"

I followed her to the ovens two aisles away. Sophie removed several dozen long, crusty baguettes and placed them on cooling racks. The smell of the fresh bread almost made me forget my ice cream.

The back door to the kitchen swung open, and I heard the sound of heels on the floor. "Who's that?" I whispered.

Sophie sighed and wrapped a small towel around one of the baguettes. "The director. Anytime I bake bread, she appears. I always make an extra loaf for her."

The silver-haired queen of McMurdo Station grimaced when she saw me. I held up my hands, flashing the universal sign of someone who has done no wrong. She accepted the bread, thanked Sophie, and pointed the skinny loaf at me. "I'm still watching you three. Don't forget it."

Once she'd left, Sophie pulled a pair of stools from under a counter and slid one to me. "It's nice to be on her good side, *oui*? Would you like some bread?"

"I was serious about the ice cream."

"Americans," she grumbled. "This is your problem!"

I shrugged, and she returned a moment later with a depressingly small bowl. I thanked her anyway. "Okay, Sophie. What's the story? Tell me everything."

135

# 10

# THE UNDERSIDE
# OF THE ICE

**ACK IN THE ROOM, AVA WAS BENT OVER THE LAPTOP,** studying the video in slow motion. While Matt, head down in concentration, walked circles around the table, Hank stood in a corner, tapping a beat on his chin with the fingers of his right hand. Britney wasn't there. Sophie and I waited in the doorway.

I coughed.

No reaction.

Mentally, Matt was still stuck on that upside-down snowstorm. "What if, like Britney said, it's some kind of biological waste material?" he asked. "Something an organism on the bottom is releasing. That makes sense, right?"

"Yes, yes, yes," Hank said. Then he stopped drumming. "No, no, no. The underside of the ice sheet would be covered in the waste material if that were the case. Yet in the video we clearly see"—he took the mouse and rewound the clip to a point that showed a view of the ice sheet from below—"that the ceiling is pure and clear. Translucent."

"So, then, it has to be ice," Matt said. "Like I suggested before."

Like he suggested? That was totally my idea.

Hank was about to respond, when his expression transformed into a curious scowl. His nose lifted upward. "What is that delectable scent? Fresh bread?" he asked.

Finally the threesome noticed us.

Sophie tossed him the heel of a baguette. "I would have brought more, but I thought Americans only liked ice cream."

Hank lifted the chunk to his nose and inhaled. "A properly prepared baguette is truly a thing of wonder. If we ever were to make contact with an intelligent extraterrestrial race, I'd argue that the baguette should be presented as an example of one of our species's greatest foods. Naturally, the food would have to be something vegetable- or grain-based. Meat or fish would be out of the question, as the aliens might be offended by our willingness to slaughter complex life forms like tuna and cows merely for the sake of protein."

"You don't like beef?" Sophie asked.

"No, I do," Hank said, "but I'm talking about aliens now. Because you see—"

"Uh, Hank?" Ava interrupted. "Jack just turned up

137

at our door with a baker. I'm thinking maybe there's a reason?"

"Right, right. Come in, come in," Hank said, closing the door behind us. "And you are?"

"Sophie Bornholdt," she said. "A chef."

"And a friend of Anna," I added.

"You're friends with Dr. Donatelli?" Hank asked. "I'm Henry Witherspoon. Hank."

"Ah, yes, the famous Hank. And you must be Ava and Matthew," she said.

I waited for Matt to glare at me, but he didn't even react. "Where's Britney?" I asked.

"She went to talk to the director," Ava said. "She's going to see if they'll organize a search for Anna."

Matt breathed out heavily. "She didn't recognize anything from the video, though, so even if she can convince the director, I don't know if they'll have any luck."

"Well, you wouldn't believe what I learned from Sophie," I said.

"Tell us, tell us," Hank said. "I'm listening."

"I would," I replied, "but I think you're going to want to see these little guys for yourself."

"Little guys? What are you talking about?"

"Anna did bring back a few sample creatures, like Levokin said. She just didn't store them in the lab. She left them with Sophie so that no one would steal them," I explained.

"But Anna told Levokin they'd been stolen," Ava noted.

"Yes, well, on the night she disappeared, I had just moved the creatures from one fridge to another, on the other side of the kitchen," Sophie said. "The first one was too busy. Too many people used it. I worried Anna's babies would be used in a stew."

"But if she couldn't find them, wouldn't she just ask you?"

With the tip of her shoe Sophie traced a circle on the floor. "I don't think she could find me. I was in the theater, watching a movie."

Sophie hadn't told me this before. "Watching a movie?" I asked. "Why didn't she just find you when it was over?"

Covering her face with her hands, Sophie mumbled her reply.

"What? I can't understand you."

She dropped her hands and cried, "It was a movie about a little dog! A Chihuahua. So cute. With a little accent. This little dog goes on these big adventures . . ." She sighed. "I watched this film three times in a row. That is why Anna could not find me. But you cannot tell anyone, okay? I'm French. We invented cinema. Watching this movie is like eating a hot-dog roll instead of a baguette."

"And you ate three hot-dog rolls," Ava said.

"*Exactement!* I was in the theater so long, poor Anna had no idea where I was. She would never think to look for me in a Chihuahua movie, and when she couldn't find her creatures, she must have thought they were stolen."

Matt was rubbing his forehead with the back of his wrist. "What do they look like, Jack? How big are they?"

"The size of my hand, maybe?" I said. "They're eerie. Freaky."

"Where are they now?" Hank asked.

"Still in the kitchen," I said.

Hank took off down the hall at the speed of an Olympic sprinter. I just stood there, stunned. I guess I'd never really seen him run. Then Matt followed—and promptly tripped on the edge of a rug.

For a moment I felt sorry for my athletically challenged sibling. He stood up and glared at me. He almost looked surprised to see that I wasn't laughing. Then he bolted after Hank.

"Should we catch up?" Ava asked.

"No, let the boys run," Sophie said. "They will wait for us. They do not know where in the kitchen to look. I could have yelled to them, but in life it is always better to have people wait for you, *mes amies*."

"*Votre conseil est bon,*" Ava responded.

*"Magnifique!"* Sophie responded. "She speaks French," she said to me.

"I know."

Hank and Matt were panting when we arrived at the kitchen door. Sophie led us inside. We were a few steps away from the fridge when she stopped. "What is this?" she asked. She crouched over a small puddle. "Jack, this is new, yes?"

She yanked open the fridge doors. The space on the shelf that had held the plastic container was depressingly vacant.

"They're gone," I said. "The creatures are gone!"

"But we left for only five minutes! How is this possible? Who would even know about them?" Sophie asked.

The director, maybe. She'd been in the kitchen recently for a baguette. But why would she steal Anna's findings? Why would she try to stop any scientific advances? That would make no sense. There was, however, another possibility. "What about Britney?" I asked. "You said she'd just left the room before Sophie and I showed up. How long ago was that?"

"It's not Britney, Jack," Hank said. "She's a geoscientist. Anna's work is totally outside her field."

Ava was down at the far end of the aisle. She pointed to a trail of small puddles on the floor. "Whoever it was went this way," she said. The thief had grabbed the container and hurried off, splashing water. We followed the trail to the end of the aisle, around the corner, and out a rear exit.

141

Outside, the hallway branched off in three directions. And there wasn't another puddle in sight.

"What now?" Ava asked.

No one answered.

No one had any clue what to do next.

The five of us wandered back to the fridge. I grabbed a towel and started drying the puddles on the floor.

"I don't understand," Hank said. "She told you to store the creatures in the fridge?"

"And they were alive?" Matt added.

"Yes, they were alive, and she was very clear in her instructions," Sophie explained. "I was to keep the fridge just below freezing. About negative one, usually."

"Celsius," I noted.

"Of course," she said. "Is there another way to measure temperature?" Hank did his I-told-you-so thing with his eyebrows. "So," Sophie continued, "negative one degree, and I was to check the little creatures once every six hours. I would scoop out the little icicles and transfer them into a separate jar. Then I would pour new water into the container with her creatures, from different jugs."

"Why?" Ava asked.

Sophie shrugged. *"Je ne sais pas."*

"I think I know," Matt said. "But I need the water to be certain."

Sophie swung open the fridge door. She grabbed a jar, then dug another one out from the cabinet beneath the steel countertop. "The thief did not find these worth stealing, I guess."

Matt read the Sharpie-drawn labels. "One says goat vinegar, and the other says . . . pig drool?"

"This was my idea. Good, no? If I labeled them 'rare creature experiment' or something like that, they might not be so easy to disguise. But nobody is interested in pig drool. Or not here, anyway. Maybe some restaurants, they could boil it down, make a sauce—"

Ava snapped her fingers. The trick was rude but effective. Sophie stopped rambling and explained the procedure that Anna had instructed her to follow. She removed the spoon I'd seen her use earlier that evening and went through the motions as if the creatures and their plastic home were still right there. "So I would take the icicles from the container and pour them into here," she said, tapping the lid of the jar labeled goat vinegar. "Then I would fill up the container with water from one of these jars."

"The pig-drool jars," Ava said.

"*Exactement.* Every six hours. For three days now. Which is why I have these little circles under my eyes."

Matt grabbed one of the pig-drool jars.

"No," Hank said. "I should be the one. Just in case it's

143

not what we think." He lifted it to his lips and poured in a mouthful. Then he swished it around and spat into the sink.

"Seawater?" Matt asked.

"Seawater," Hank said. He winced. "That's cold. Hurt-your-teeth cold."

Hank didn't stop my brother when he screwed the lid off the next Mason jar—the "goat vinegar"—and drank. "Wow. Amazing. Perfectly fresh."

I was about to interrupt, when Sophie asked the question for me. "Would one of you please explain what is happening?"

"Don't you see?" Matt asked.

No, we did not.

"The creatures were desalinating the seawater!" Hank said.

"Like the Clutterbuck Prize," I said.

"That's right, Jack," Matt said. He sounded genuinely surprised.

Hank began walking in small circles. "This is amazing. World-changing! Huge. Beyond huge. Cosmic!" He stopped. "Well, maybe not cosmic. But huge. Really."

Matt was practically bouncing with excitement. "Those freaky little creatures you saw must be able to ingest, or drink in, the seawater, then separate the salt from the water. The output is salt and freshwater."

"So they suck in saltwater and excrete fresh, drinkable

water," Hank added. "But it freezes instantly in the subzero water, forming those little icicles."

Okay, so I'm pretty good with words, and I knew what excrete meant. That's the way our bodies, or the bodies of any organism, get rid of the stuff they don't want. Normally we "excrete" into a white ceramic bowl that has a plumbing system linked to the back. "So if those creatures excreted that freshwater, Matt, then you just drank their pee."

Hank was too excited to notice the joke. "Exactly!" he said. "Try some! It's delicious."

Ava and Sophie chuckled.

"Jack, this is serious," Matt said. "This discovery is enormous. I mean, if you were to use these creatures, or maybe design a machine that copies the way they work, you could make clean drinking water for tens of millions of people."

145

Maybe it was his mention of millions, but an idea hit me immediately. I rushed it out before anyone else expressed the same thought. "Someone who did that could win the Clutterbuck Prize. Right?"

Everyone was quiet for a moment. I was right. I could see it in their faces, in the way Hank drummed his fingers on his chin. Anna's disappearance wasn't just about science anymore. Her discovery was also worth real money. We were talking about a million dollars to start. And likely far more to come. Now any number of people could have tried to steal her creatures. Levokin, Golding, even that cranky, silver-haired director. Had she really left the kitchen after grabbing her baguette? Or had she hidden in the next aisle, listening to Sophie explain everything? Maybe she was the culprit all along. Or maybe Hank was wrong, and our friend Britney had tricked us all into believing she was on our side.

Ava squeezed my shoulder. "The stickycams!" she yelled.

"Sticky what?" Sophie asked.

We didn't stop to explain. Both Ava and I dashed out through the back door of the kitchen. The others followed. Across the hall, only a few paces away, one of Ava's miniature cameras was lodged in the space between an exit sign and the wall. Whoever stole the creatures would've had to rush right past that camera. Ava was impatiently tapping at the screen of her smartphone.

"Anything?" I asked.

"I have to wait for it to sync."

A few seconds later Ava had the video running on her tiny screen. The picture was not as clear as I'd hoped. The lens was fogged; Hank guessed that the warm, humid air flowing out of the kitchen was to blame. But then Ava found what we'd been hoping for: a short video clip of someone racing out the back kitchen door, carrying a plastic container. You couldn't see the person's face. But that wasn't necessary. The thief was wearing an offensively bright orange jacket.

# 11
# CIRCLE MARKS THE SPOT

**D**O THEY HAVE SPECIAL PRISONS FOR CHEATING scientists? Probably not. But if they did, I imagine the calculators would all be out of batteries, the protractors would be broken, and the inmates would never be allowed outside, since even a cloudy day can be interesting to a scientist. There had to be some kind of fitting punishment for Franklin Golding, the man who was too good to wear a Big Red like everyone else. I was awake half the night imagining what would happen when we caught him and Anna was safely returned.

The night before, we'd started searching for Golding, asking dozens of people if they'd seen him. The Facilities Engineer didn't know if he'd returned from his last outing. Walter had no clue. None of Sophie's friends on the dining staff remembered seeing the golden boy around lately. Britney found us outside Hank's room at one point. She said she'd failed to convince the director to search for Anna, and she had no idea whether Golding was around, either. Eventually Matt stopped a sweat-soaked Victor Valenza on his way back from the gym, and the diver insisted that our suspect was still in the field.

"You will soon see for yourself," he'd said. "They're sending a helicopter tomorrow to pick him up. Maybe you can talk this crew into looking for Anna, too. The east side of the ice shelf offers the best diving—it's full of aquatic life. That's why Golding is there in the first place."

I didn't know whether to believe him. But one way or another, we had to get on that helicopter.

When Hank opened the door to our room the next morning, he immediately declared that I looked terrible. My mouth felt like it had been blown dry, and the skin around my knuckles was starting to crack. Matt was at the desk, reading. I sat up and reached for a glass of water as Ava, up and about, followed Hank inside. She was wearing the pink fleece. Instantly my mood brightened. As expected, she had run out of clean clothes, and I'd been only too happy to give her the secret stash I'd packed. But my victory wasn't complete until that moment. She saw the joy on my face and scowled. "Don't say a word," she said.

I coughed and drank. After our chat with Valenza, Hank had promised to work on the director to let us go on the helicopter trip. "What's the plan?" I asked. "Are we going?"

"We're going," he said.

"How did you convince her?" Matt asked.

"Simple. She said she'd let us on the helicopter if we agreed to leave Antarctica on an earlier flight than we'd planned."

Sometimes it was good to be despised. "Did you talk to the pilots? Did they agree to search the area for Anna?"

Hank nodded. "It's all set. We'll fly east of Golding's camp, closer to the Ross Ice Shelf. They said we should be able to cover a lot of ice. Then we'll circle back to pick him up."

What was Golding going to do when we found her? Lie? Deny his involvement? Pretend he knew nothing? I couldn't wait to see how he'd react. Part of me hoped he'd sob a little.

Hank squinted at me, sticking his chin out. "Are you sure you're up for this trip?"

My attempted response failed, and I coughed up something that looked like one of Anna's creatures. "Of course," I said.

After I got dressed, we ate, bundled up in our Big Reds, and rushed out to the helicopter pad. The blades were spinning slowly, just enough to kick up thin clouds of snow. An official from the medical center stood waiting outside the doors.

The official gave everyone a quick inspection before letting us past, and I prodded Ava and Matt to go first. When it was my turn, our examiner's eyes narrowed. She leaned to one side, studying me. "Cough," she said.

"I'm fine."

"Cough."

I faked one. "Sorry, I can't."

She clapped me on the back. A slick lump flew up out of my lungs and into my mouth. "Spit it out," she said, pointing to the ground. And I did. A nasty yellow-brown chunk splattered onto the hard dirt. She kneeled and studied it briefly. "You're staying here. In bed."

There was probably no point arguing, but I did anyway.

I lost.

Hank tried to look disappointed. "Health comes first with small humans, right? Maybe you can catch up on your schoolwork, too. And don't worry about Anna." He patted me on the shoulder. "We'll find her."

"I'm sorry," Ava said.

But her sympathy wasn't getting me onto that helicopter. All the excitement and energy drained from my body like water out of a tub. Look, I've been abandoned before. Five times, at least; that's not even counting the first and most important time, since back then I was only an infant. But this stung like an arrow to my heart. I was the one who had thought there was something weird about Anna's disappearance. I had annoyed everyone until they'd listened.

Sure, I'd forgotten to check the e-mail, but I'd made them take this whole thing seriously. And now they were going off to save her. Without me. They were going to be the heroes, while I sat back at the base.

Watching the helicopter lift off would've been too painful, so I moped back to our room. I checked my home-school assignments on the computer for about a minute, then flopped back onto my bed. The stack of Anna's research papers that Hank had printed for Matt lay on the floor. I hadn't read them yet. But I was tired of thinking about her. As soon as I laid down and closed my eyes, though, a movie started playing in my brain. I could see Ava spotting Anna's shelter from the helicopter, and the group of them swooping down to rescue her. There would be tears, cheers, celebration.

I sat up. The stack of papers was taunting me. I wanted to forget all about Anna for a while, but instead I started skimming through the papers. Thankfully it wasn't just research. There were also articles from magazines, including a few interviews, and it looked like Matt hadn't even touched these. One had appeared in *Popular Science* magazine nearly ten years earlier. There was a reference to that meteorite-hunting trip Hank had mentioned. She talked about her education, her theories, her goals. And halfway down the second page of the interview I nearly shouted with surprise. I read her words twice to make sure I wasn't imagining them.

*PS: Were you always interested in extreme life-forms?*

*AD: My first love was science fiction. Jules Verne in particular.* Twenty Thousand Leagues Under the Sea *was my bible.*

The interview went on, but that was all I needed. I jumped up and raced to the library. Several grumpy staffers told me to slow down. One of the rugs that had tripped Matt nearly grabbed me as well, but I threw a hand up against the wall for balance and kept running.

The library was small and old-fashioned. Overstuffed shelves lined the walls, and a card catalog cabinet stood in one corner. A few comfortable chairs were arranged in the center of the room. The Facilities Engineer was lounging with a paperback in his lap, filing his fingernails. Did the nail dust land in the book? Did he even care? Over the tops of his thin eyeglasses he glanced at me. "Greetings, Earthling," he said.

"They have science fiction here, right?" I asked.

He pointed his thumb to a section of the shelves diagonally behind him. "Back there."

The science-fiction section was huge, and Verne was there in strong numbers. At least ten of his works, in fact. I finger-walked over the spines. Stuck between two thoroughly used copies of *Twenty Thousand Leagues Under the Sea* was a thin, leather-bound book with no title. I removed it, and the cover was bare except for two letters in gold. Initials, to be precise. *A* and *D*. My heart beat faster.

The notes inside were all in Italian. Even if I had known how to read the language, I'm not sure I could've made sense of her jottings. Her handwriting was absolutely horrendous. My third-grade teacher, Mrs. Cuneo, probably would've sent me back to kindergarten if she'd caught me writing like that. I flipped through slowly until a large, thick piece of paper, folded over several times, fell to the floor.

"Careful," the F. E. whispered.

Had he been watching me? I glanced at him. He was still reading and filing. I leaned down and partially unfolded the paper. The only sound in the room was the steady, scratchy sanding of fingernails. My heart was thumping. But the sketch in my hands was clearly a map. I couldn't believe it. Had I actually found it? I slipped the paper back into the notebook, took a copy of the Verne novel, and held it over the notebook.

I was on my way when the F. E. called to me again. "You do have to check that out, you know," he said.

153

"Now you're a librarian?"

"Watch your tone, kid," he snapped back. "And, yes, in the mornings, I am a librarian, and in the afternoons I'm the Facilities Engineer. Just write the title, your name, and today's date on that sign-out sheet."

I dashed out the details, grabbed *Twenty Thousand Leagues* and the leather journal, and hustled back to the room. Once the door was closed, I spread the drawing out on my bed. The map covered an enormous square roughly one hundred miles on a side. Our location—Ross Island, with McMurdo Station at its southern tip—was penciled in near the lower right corner. The coast of mainland Antarctica started all the way on the right side, about halfway up, then dipped down underneath Ross Island and curved up again to the left and toward the top. I tilted my head. The coast looked kind of like a backward *J*. And in the spots where ice covered the sea, which was most of the bottom half of the map, Anna had drawn dashed parallel lines.

The mountains of the mainland, part of the Transantarctic range, stretched from the top to the bottom of the map on the left side. The volcano was on the right side, in the middle of Ross Island. And this is where it got interesting. Near the Transantarctic Mountains, along the coast, Anna had drawn a series of circles. She'd sketched them with a fine-tipped green pen and slashed several of them through with a red *X*. One cluster of markings was between McMurdo and the mainland—no more than five or ten miles from the base. All of these had been x-ed out in red. They must have been the sites she'd explored with Levokin and their team, the ones that she was actually approved to visit. After that, as Levokin explained, she'd snuck away to explore more-distant locations.

The green circles extended up the left side of the page, along the coast, and the red *X*s continued until the northernmost spot marked on the map. More than halfway up the coast was a final green circle. I leaned back. That had to be the spot. But if those were the sites she'd been exploring, then there was another problem. The helicopter crew was searching the area east of Ross Island. That meant they were looking in the wrong place.

155

I stared at the final green circle. Was that where Anna had found the creatures? She probably could have gotten there on a snowmobile, when she ditched Levokin and crew, but now she was on her own. The Mechanical Equipment Center had no record of a missing snowmobile, either, so she didn't have a vehicle. Was it even possible to travel that far on foot?

I tore a piece of paper from a notebook, then laid it along the bottom of Anna's map. The notepaper was exactly half as wide, lining up with the fold in the middle of the map. According to Anna's key, the map represented about one hundred miles on a side. That meant the crease mark, and the width of my notebook paper, was a distance of fifty miles. I folded my paper. The crease in the middle marked out twenty-five miles. Then I folded it twice more, to mark out twelve-and-a-half and six-something. (Give me a break, okay? I didn't have my calculator with me. And by that I mean Ava.) I wrote out all the distances and aligned the edge of the page with Anna's circles.

My system wasn't exact. But each of those circles looked to be roughly ten miles apart. I measured all the way up to the uppermost unmarked circle and added up the distance. But the number was too large. That would be impossible. I checked my math, adding the sum again. And I found the same answer. So if that map was right, then the last site Anna explored was nearly fifty miles north up the coast of Antarctica. Was she really that crazy? Would she really try to march fifty miles through the snow to find more of those creatures?

I sat back. I was desperate to tell someone. But until we confirmed that it was Franklin Golding trying to steal Anna's discovery, I couldn't risk it. What if I was wrong and spilled everything to the real villain? All I could do now was wait for the others to return. I ordered a small pepperoni pizza to the room. I drank about fifteen glasses of water. And I waited.

And waited.

And waited.

That was probably the second longest day of my life. The first? The time my foster father Herb took me deer hunting when I was six years old. We went out into the woods before sunrise, climbed up into this tiny wooden house on stilts, and sat there for ten hours looking for deer. I was cold, tired, and cosmically bored. I don't like the idea of killing a defenseless animal, but by noon I was ready to jump out of that shack and put Bambi in a chokehold if it would get me home a few minutes earlier. Still, Herb wasn't a bad dad. He'd tried. And I might've stuck around with him and Marie if they hadn't gotten busted for running an online gambling ring.

Anyway, time did move forward, and when the helicopter finally returned, I was so anxious, I dashed outside to meet the group without fully zipping up my Big Red. The cold swept through my few thin layers of clothing and wrapped its frigid hands around my ribs. My nostrils froze solid, and I raced back inside before I even had a chance to wave.

Ava and Matt hurried in first.

"What took you so long?" I asked.

"Long?" Matt said. "We're back three hours early."

Ava shook a little as she unzipped her coat. A thin layer of frost had formed around the tops of her eyebrows. "Aren't you going to ask if we found her?"

157

"No."

"Why not?" Matt asked.

"Because I already know you were looking in the wrong place."

Ava crossed her arms on her chest, striking a thoroughly doubtful pose. "You do?"

Now I lowered my voice to a whisper and patted my chest, where I'd hidden the folded paper. "I found her map."

Matt nearly choked. "Really?"

"Really."

Ava's eyes widened. "Seriously?"

Was it really so hard to believe I'd succeeded? "Yes! I'm serious!"

Another blast of wind screamed through as the door opened again. At the other end of the room, Hank and a handsome blond man stomped their feet on the floor. "That's Golding, right?" I asked.

"It is," Matt answered.

For some reason our enemy was wearing a Big Red. "Where's his orange jacket?" I whispered. "And how was he out there if we saw him here on the video last night?"

"That's the thing," Ava said. "He claims he's been out at the dive site since the day after we got here. And he says he lost his orange jacket right before he left."

"He's lying."

"Or someone's trying to frame him," Matt said. "I don't know if Golding's our guy anymore, Jack. I mean, how would he have gotten back to the base for one night? Plus he and Hank are basically best friends already."

"That doesn't mean he's innocent. Hank likes anyone who can talk science or engineering."

"What was that?" Hank asked. "Jack, how are you feeling? Better? You didn't miss anything. Not a sign of Anna. But Dr. Golding here believes we were looking in the wrong spot."

"Really?" I asked.

Golding pulled off his gloves and rubbed his face. "She was obsessed with the coastline," he said. "Right along the mainland, northeast of here."

"But . . ." My words faded. I didn't know what to say. Why was he telling us the right place to look?

He rubbed his face again. "I hope she has a good shelter," he said. "This is going to be a serious storm." With a quick wave Golding left us, pulling off his Big Red as he walked down the hall.

"Storm?" I asked. "What storm?"

"That's why we hurried back early," said Hank. "There's a massive Herbie coming off the mainland. They're making everyone within ten miles come back to McMurdo and get inside before nightfall."

159

"I know where she is," I said. Hank listened closely as I described my discovery. "We have to tell the helicopter crew to go back out."

"The director isn't going to let anyone off the base," Hank said. "Not even the search and rescue team. We're just going to have to hope Anna is prepared."

"This is crazy!" I said. "We have to help her."

"Believe me, Jack, I know!" Hank said. "But no one is leaving the base today."

"She'll be able to ride it out," Matt said.

Ava nodded in agreement, as if she were trying to convince herself. "She's strong."

An avalanche of ideas and emotions tumbled through my head in the next few instants. Then I took a long, slow breath, forced a smile, and patted my brother on the back. "You're right, Matt. Ava."

Hank exhaled. He stared at the floor for a moment, then looked up. He mumbled that he had something to do, then left us without explanation. We started back to our room. Halfway there, Matt grabbed my shoulder. I stopped. "What?" I asked.

"You never admit it when I'm right," he noted.

Ava shrugged. "It's true. You don't."

Matt swiped some imaginary dust off his shoulder.

"Then you added that weird pat on the back. You never do that, either. What's going on?"

I paused. I'd been hoping for a little more time to figure out how to sell them my plan.

"Jack?" Ava said. "What is it?"

"Well . . . you see, I was wondering . . . Matt, do you think you can drive one of those trucks we looked at during Happy Camper training? The ones in the Mechanical Equipment Center?"

Matt's face paled. He looked at me sideways. "Maybe?"

"Good."

"This is not just a hypothetical question, is it?" Ava asked.

"No, it's not," I answered. "We're not going to leave Anna out there in this storm."

"We're not?" Matt asked.

"No," I said. "We're going to go get her ourselves."

161

# 12

# THE WORST IDEA EVER

Y BROTHER AND SISTER SPENT THE NEXT TEN minutes detailing why my latest brainchild was dangerous, impossible, foolish, and completely ridiculous. The director would kick us off the continent. We'd be stripped of our status as legal adults. Hank would refuse to work with us again. Min would abandon us. And so on and so on. I sort of listened, but I was also busily building my counterattack. We'd done a unit on persuasive writing in my homeschooling program last year, and the instructor I'd had to video-chat with was always talking about how the key to developing a strong argument is understanding your weak points. In this case, my siblings were right about the logical side of my proposal. There was not much sense to what I'd suggested. So I would appeal to their hearts instead of their heads.

When my turn to talk finally arrived, I asked them both to imagine what it was like to be Anna. Ava had been adjusting one of Fred's antennas. Tinkering with electronics helps her think, so I asked her to stop. "Really imagine it," I said.

"Jack, I don't think—"

"Please, just hear me out. Hands off the robot."

"Fine."

"Think about it," I began. "She's a maverick. A brave woman struggling to succeed in a field dominated by men. But she keeps pushing. Diving deeper and longer than anyone has ever dared. Yet she still doesn't find anything. So the doubts start creeping in more and more, like a virus. But she doesn't give up. She pushes further. She goes farther and farther out into that frozen landscape, searching for undersea creatures. She's also searching for her soul," I stared at the floor for a moment. Looking at one of them might break my flow. "Then, long after most sane people would have given up, she finds them. The groundbreaking life forms she's spent her whole career searching for. Her whole life, in a way, was leading up to this one discovery." I paused. This piece was for Matt, and I needed it to latch on. "And then someone steals that breakthrough. They steal her creatures. They even dare to steal her computer." I paused again, shaking my head, letting that particular loss sink in with Ava. "So she races back out into the cold, frozen wasteland to save her reputation, her creatures, maybe even her soul.

And does anyone help her? No. Because we're too afraid of a little storm." My intensity was even getting to me now. My voice was rising. My heart was beating faster. "Was Shackleton afraid of bad weather? Was Amundsen? Or Scott? No, they—"

"Jack?" Matt interrupted.

"—they didn't care about wind and snow. They traveled hundreds of miles across this frigid landscape, and they didn't have giant warm vehicles or Big Reds! They shot puppies and ate penguin cutlets to survive. They didn't have modern technology. All they had—"

"Jack, honestly, we—"

"All they had was a powerful mixture of curiosity and courage and—"

"JACK!" Matt shouted.

Ava plunked a pencil eraser off my ear.

A quick glance at the two of them confirmed what I'd suspected. "We're good?" I asked.

"Yeah, we're good," Ava said. "You had me at the stolen computer."

"And me at the theft of her discovery," Matt added.

He took the map from my hands and spread it out on the table. I started to explain my measuring system, but he estimated the distance on sight. "About fifty-one miles, I'd say."

"Exactly," I said. "We can do it tonight, during the big karaoke contest."

"All the way up there and back?"

"That's right. A quick road trip."

Ava ran her hand along Shelly's yellow exterior. "Can I bring her?"

"Of course!" I said. "You totally have to test her."

They were both quiet, staring down at the map. Was that it? Had I convinced them that easily?

Matt backed away. "No, I don't like it. I don't like it at all. I've never driven more than twenty minutes. Now you want me to drive all night? How am I even supposed to stay awake?"

"I'll sing," I suggested.

"What Jack means is that we'll stay up with you," Ava promised. "Without singing."

Matt shook his head rapidly. "The PistenBully is too slow. We'll never make it there and back in a night."

"We wouldn't take a PistenBully," I said. And I didn't have to say which vehicle I had in mind.

"You're not thinking about the Rambler, are you? That's the director's baby! You heard what they said during Happy Camper."

"She doesn't even like people breathing on that truck," Ava added.

165

"It's the only one that could fit all of us and get us back by morning. If we want to save Anna, the Rambler is our only choice."

Matt flopped back on his bed and stared at the ceiling. I was going to continue, but Ava lifted a finger to her lips. Let him think, the gesture said. So I did, and after a moment of silence Matt sat up again. "See, the only thing is, I don't want to get caught," he said.

"None of us do, but—"

"Jack, let me talk, okay? I don't want to get caught, because I want to get invited back someday. This place . . ." He shook his head, smiling. "This is the most amazing place I've ever been. I'd come back here every year if I could. But if we get caught sneaking off the base in the middle of the night, during a storm, there's no way they'll ever let me return."

"I'll take the blame." I spun around. Hank stood in the doorway. "Nice speech, Jack. We may have to make a senator out of you."

This was no time for flattery, but I quietly savored the comment. "What do you mean, you'll take the blame?"

"If we're caught, I'll say it was all my idea. I don't mind being kicked out of here, to be honest. The environment is fascinating, but it's simply too cold. You were right, Jack. Tahiti really would have been a nicer spot for the Clutterbuck

Prize. Still, I do understand your passion, Matt, and the last thing I want to do is jeopardize your ability to return."

"But we have to get Anna," Ava said, surprising me.

"Agreed. We can't leave her out there another night. Borrowing the Rambler would be a terrible decision, though, so we will have to use another means of transportation."

"We?"

"Yes, we," Hank said. "I'm driving."

Ava actually bounced across the room and hugged him. Matt started to do the same, then stuck out his hand and modified the embrace into what Hank calls the one-arm-guy-hug. It's an expression of affection common among young and adult men. They hold their right hands out, with their arms bent at right angles, clasp those hands together, then lean in and pat each other on the back with their left hands. It's more of a half hug, really. And Matt had only recently come to master it.

I remained at the desk. This was good news but hardly a reason to celebrate. "However we get there, we'll need to slip away without anyone knowing. Whoever's been trying to steal Anna's work definitely won't want us finding her. We need a good distraction."

"The karaoke contest will help. Golding will draw a crowd."

"We need more than a regular crowd."

The sound of Evgeny Levokin's voice floated through my mind. "What if we bill it as Golding against the Russian?"

They let the idea hover for a moment before Ava answered. "You heard Evgeny in our shelter that night. He never even goes to the contests. And there's still a chance he could be part of this whole thing . . . he never did say exactly what he's submitting for the Clutterbuck Prize."

"Certainly suspicious," Hank said.

"Ava and I will convince him to compete."

"We will? How?"

"I have an idea."

"Okay," Matt said. "If you say so. What am I supposed to do?"

"You come with me," Hank said to Matt. "We have a few tests to run before the trip."

We split up, and by dinnertime, the showdown was all anyone could talk about. Ava and I had made up boxing-match-style posters with Golding's face on one side and Levokin's on the other. We billed it as the battle of the century. The Russian Lullaby versus the Golden Boy. As part of our scheme to distract the director, we also noted in large lettering that there would be free baguettes—so Sophie was essential. For two hours we plastered our posters all across McMurdo Station. At one point, Angelo, our Happy Camper instructor, stopped me while I was taping one outside the director's office and offered to help post more.

Ava and I were at the door to the basketball court when someone coughed behind us. A deep, rumbling sort of cough that could have come from only one person. Slowly I turned around. Levokin's huge eyebrows were scrunched together. "You did this, yes?"

"Yes," Ava answered.

"I do not wish to compete."

"Golding said he's going to flatten you," I lied. "He said you have the voice of a dying bear."

Levokin snorted.

"It's true," Ava added. "He said listening to you sing will be like listening to an elephant seal trying to cover Taylor Swift."

That was all the man needed to hear. He added another snort, then finished with an emphatic grunt. "I do not sound like seal! I hate nothing more than seals! Where is this impersonator? This fool! I will beat him now. I will take his pretty blond hair and twist it around—"

"Wait, no!" Ava said. "You're going to fight him? That wasn't—"

Levokin waved both hands in the air. "No, no, no. I was speaking . . . with metaphor? Yes. Metaphor. I will beat him like this with my voice." He massaged his throat and closed his eyes. A few low notes emerged, and he ascended to an impossibly high pitch. Then he coughed. He shook his head. "No, tonight is impossible. I have cold."

Suddenly I felt hollow. If the Russian had the crud, I could see only one way to get him to compete. It would require a great personal sacrifice. And yet it had to be done. I reached into my pocket, removed Hank's greatest contribution to the world, and held it out to him. "This should help," I said.

Levokin needed no instructions. He untwisted the steel cap and lifted the vacuum to his nose. The slurping sound that followed was revolting. Ava looked ready to vomit. But then he sang a few notes, and the sound of his voice was magical.

He tried to give me back the vacuum. "No," I said, figuring Hank would not mind. "It's yours. Really."

Levokin held it up and shook his head. "I will not forget this, my little friend. Tonight I will be ready. Make sure they have the Billy Joel."

An hour before the start of the karaoke contest, the crowd was already growing at Gallagher's Pub, the site of the showdown. Outside the cafeteria I heard Danno trying to convince the Facilities Engineer that he was better than either Levokin or Golding. We bumped into Britney, too, and I could see in Ava's eyes that she wanted to tell her about our plan. But even if Britney was innocent, she'd never let us go out in that storm. I gently stepped on my sister's toes to keep her quiet.

Luckily, Victor Valenza interrupted us before Ava could give anything away. He was warming up for the contest. Unfortunately, he made us listen to him rap. To spare you the pain, I won't repeat his rhymes in full, but here's a sample:

*I love deep divin'*
*Ice water jivin'*
*No matter how cold*
*I'm always survivin'.*

And, yes, it was as bad as it sounds.

Besides the rapping diver, everything was moving along smoothly. Ava and I had already stuffed together several emergency packs in case we got stuck out there in the Herbie. We had a few dozen chocolate bars, several days' worth of dried food, and twelve cold slices of leftover pepperoni pizza. We'd amassed a collection of sleeping bags, tents, shovels, and almost every other kind of survival gear you could imagine. Plus we had Shelly and Fred all ready to go. The only problem? We hadn't seen Hank or Matt for hours, so we still didn't know if we had a vehicle.

# 13
# SNOWGOING

**INNER WAS OVER A LITTLE BEFORE NINE, AT ABOUT**
the same time the contest was set to start. Ava and I
remained at our table until the cafeteria was empty.
The door to the kitchen opened, and Sophie leaned
out. *"Commençons-nous maintenant?"* she asked.

"*Oui,*" Ava replied. Then she looked at me. "Operation
*La Baguette* is a go."

That's not what we'd agreed to call it. And I wasn't thinking of it as a French mission, but I let it slide, since Hank
and Matt had finally returned. My brother's face was pale;
he was scratching at his hip and standing awkwardly. Hank
was jittery.

"Are we all set?" I asked. "Did you find us a ride?"

"More than a ride," Hank replied with a wink.

"So . . . yes?"

After a brief pause Hank answered, "Yes, yes. We are
ready."

The four of us just stood there. No one smiled, and there was a heaviness to the moment. If we were in a movie, music would've been playing. A quiet, steady beat building in intensity. What were we doing? What were the four of us, exactly? In a strange way, we were starting to feel like a family. A really unusual, multicolored, mixed-up unit, but a family all the same.

Someone should've said something.

Instead, I lifted my wrist and tapped the face of an imaginary watch. "Okay," I said, "it's go time."

We split up to finish our jobs, and at eight minutes past nine o'clock, Ava and I arrived at the entrance to Gallagher's Pub, the regular site of the karaoke wars. Already the room was so crowded, you couldn't squeeze inside. The heat flowing out of the space was intense, and it reeked of sweat. Ava grabbed a chair from just inside and stood on the seat, peering into the audience. "Golding?" I asked.

"Yep, he's there," she said. "Levokin, too."

"And the director?"

"That should be taken care of in a minute. The baguettes are baked."

I smiled. What she'd said sounded like some kind of coded message, you know? The eagle has landed. The train has left the station. The baguettes are baked. That sort of thing. Only we were literally talking about loaves of bread,

and a moment later my nose picked up the otherworldly aroma bursting off their golden crusts. Down the hall, Sophie was pushing a cart loaded with her creations, four or five dozen loaves in all. Each one was kicking off a scent that would make a man who had just won a hot-dog-eating contest wonder if he had room for a few more bites. Heads turned. Nostrils flared with delight. Oohs and ahs arose from the crowd. And, most important, behind the cart stalked the silver-haired director, following in a trance.

"Bingo," Ava said. "Her eyes aren't even open."

Sophie paused at the doorway. "Now?" she whispered.

"Go, go. Lead her inside."

The crowd in the doorway moved aside as Sophie pressed forward, making room where there was none, and she squeezed through into the middle of the tavern. An engineer reached for a loaf. She slapped away his hand. An oceanographer tried from the other side. A stare from Sophie's green eyes frightened him into retreating to a table. And still, there was the director, right behind her. Sophie looked back at me through the crowd. I nodded. Slowly she handed the director a loaf of bread.

On stage, the massive Russian engineer sat at a keyboard, while Golding, Valenza, and the other contestants stood waiting to one side. Levokin's eyes were closed. His head hung loosely forward, as if he were entranced. A song began to play. The Russian started to strike the keys with delicate expertise. The crowd became quiet. The director slumped into a chair with her precious bread.

And we ran.

We grabbed our Big Reds, pulled on our boots and gloves, and pushed outside into the strangely bright night. The wind was stronger than it had been earlier in the day, hitting my cheeks like a thousand tiny pinpricks. Huge swirls of snow were gathering around the mountaintops in the distance.

Down the hill, Matt and Hank stood waiting. My brother was shifting awkwardly from side to side. Our packs were there, jammed with the tents and shovels and ropes and food—enough survival gear to last a week or more. And on the snow between Matt and Hank was . . . a sled. Were they serious? Was this really the big surprise? At the very least I was hoping for a few snowmobiles. "This was your plan? A sled?"

"This is not a sled!" Hank said.

Ava's expression changed into a skeptical sneer. "This is our ride?"

"You haven't seen it in action yet," Hank said. He reached down and started fidgeting with a set of switches. A green light flicked on.

"You saw Anna's map, right?" I asked. "We're talking

176

about fifty miles!" I held out my hands, motioning to the endless desert of snow that stretched out in front of us. "Fifty miles over that! With a storm on the way! How is this thing supposed to help?"

Ava turned back toward the station. "I am not going to get stuck out there in the middle of nowhere and be forced to eat cute little penguins."

The sudden whine of an engine should have been enough to draw her back to us, but the wind drowned out the sound. I called out, "Ava?"

"I told you, I'm not—"

"Ava?" I repeated. "You might want to take a look."

That ridiculously lame sled? Well, it wasn't a sled at all. The bottom was rigid. But when Hank powered it up, that hardened shell unfolded itself several times, then snapped together again so that it doubled in length and width. Then a flexible, silvery material unfurled from the middle and began to inflate. "Is that—"

"The same material that broke your fall outside my building," Hank said with a smile. A bubblelike vehicle slowly took shape in front of our eyes, with windows all around and a flap in the back, held in place by Velcro.

Matt started to walk around the contraption. For some reason he was limping. "This is amazing," he said.

Ava was paralyzed with wonder.

177

"Go ahead," Hank said. "Check it out."

Inside, there was room in the back to stow our gear, plus four inflatable seats arranged in two rows. Between the two front seats was a control panel about the size of an iPad.

Hank pointed to a large, wide, oval-shaped opening in the rigid bottom, saying something about a turbine.

"That looks like a big mouth," I said.

"And it is! Sort of," Hank said. "Remember that snow-blower in the lab?"

"I was wondering what you were doing with that," Ava said.

"That old machine was my inspiration. The vehicle sucks up the snow here, through the mouth, then spits it out the back. That's how it propels itself."

178

"You call it the Snowgoer, don't you?" I asked.

The look of disappointment on his face was as clear as a glass of water. "Yes . . . You don't like it?"

"I love it," Ava said. "Now let's see if it really goes."

Once inside, we fought over seats. Ava won. She reached down and held up one of my missing Xbox controllers. "Look what I found!"

"Hey!" I said. "How'd that get in here?"

"Oh, I forgot to tell you," Hank said. "I borrowed it. These are very impressive little remotes. Now, keep your Big

Reds zipped up—there's no heater in here—and buckle into your safety harnesses, everyone."

Next to me, Matt was scratching above his knee. "What's wrong with your leg?" I asked.

"Nothing."

I clicked into my harness, which was like five different seat belts coming from all directions. The combination of the straps and my Big Red was uncomfortably snug. "I can barely move," I groaned.

"Perfect!" Hank said.

He flicked a few switches on the control panel. Something beneath us hummed to life. Ever so slightly the Snowgoer started to vibrate. The subtle pulsing built to a steady roar.

"Is this supposed to happen?" I yelled.

Hank pulled a pair of earmuffs on over his hood. "Yes, yes, there are a few fine points I still need to work out in the design, but she's working well. That noise is only the beginning. It's going to get LOUD!" he shouted. "Everybody, put on your earmuffs!" The three of us looked at one another and shrugged; none of us had earmuffs. "Ready?" he shouted.

The Snowgoer sucked up the soft white powder in front of us. The vehicle lurched, then found what must have been a perfect mouthful of snow, because it accelerated as if it

179

were cruising downhill, racing smoothly out across the ice. Our progress was slow at first, then ramped up to about the pace of a bicycle, and on up to that of a subway train. Hank was whooping. Ava was hollering. A smile cracked through the terror frozen onto Matt's face. And the excitement was pulsing through me in bolts, warming me against the frigid air.

The Snowgoer did not just go; we sped across that frozen terrain like we'd been launched from the world's largest slingshot. And for a while I just kicked back and enjoyed the ride.

Then, after we'd been cruising for at least half an hour, I noticed a small problem.

Far ahead on the horizon a white lump was growing larger as we approached. I leaned forward, pointed, and yelled, "What's that?"

Hank held up the Xbox controller. Over his shoulder, he cried out, "Don't worry! I'll steer around it!"

The Snowgoer veered left, but the lump stretched too far in either direction. And I knew what it was without having to see any more. In the summer, the ice shelf thinned, and cracks appeared in places. Then the plates on either side of the crack would push together, grind against each other, and crumble upward, creating mounds of ice and snow that could stretch for miles.

The lumpy and jagged ridge ahead of us now was no minor speed bump on the ice. The obstacle looked to be about as high as a basketball hoop.

"Maybe we should hit the brakes?" I asked.

"Ah, but that's one of the finer points I'm still working on," Hank called back.

"What do you mean?"

"She doesn't exactly have brakes!"

To our left was a smooth spot, the ice sloping gently upward from the surface, forming a ramp. I pointed. "There!" I shouted.

Was this good advice? Not necessarily. But one suggestion was all Hank needed. He aimed our unstoppable craft at the ramp.

181

At the last instant, just before we hit the base, I closed my eyes. The front of the Snowgoer rose, pushing me into the back of my seat. My stomach spun. Someone shouted. And as the engine roared and the yells grew louder, we became weightless. I opened my eyes. Smooth snow lay below us, clear ice ahead.

We were flying.

# 14

# A DESERT OF
# ICE AND SNOW

**UMAN FLIGHT IS AN AMAZING ACCOMPLISHMENT** when planned. The Wright Brothers, for example. The Apollo missions. Michael Jordan. But the Snowgoer was not meant to fly. Hank's vehicle was designed to travel along the surface, and as the front leaned down and to the left, I realized we were heading there quickly.

The plastic windshield struck the ice first.

The inflatable walls bent, absorbing the impact. The harness pressed harder into my stuffy coat as we flipped over.

The vehicle bumped and rolled. My brain somersaulted. My stomach did some kind of backflip. Clumps of snow were flying around inside the vehicle. But the harness held tight, and my Big-Red-wrapped body remained in my seat.

Somehow we landed upright. I spat some snow off my lip.

"Everyone okay?" Hank asked. There was a rare note of panic in his voice. "Anything broken?"

"Besides the Snowgoer? No."

Hank exhaled, massively relieved. Then he let out a few strange, excited, nonsensical whoops. "Wow! Right?" He moved his jaw as if to check whether it was still working. "There's inertia for you. I mean, I know an object in motion stays in motion unless acted upon by an outside force"—he patted the Snowgoer's inflatable sides—"but that's the first time I've actually been the object in motion."

Matt laughed; I didn't get the joke.

"Why's it so quiet?" Ava asked. "Did the motor shut down?"

Something clanked shut at the front of the vehicle. "That's the intake valve," Hank said. Then, for me, he added, "You know, the mouth. It's a crash safety feature. The vehicle shuts itself down and closes up."

"So let's start her up again," Ava said.

"We can't," Hank said. He pulled off his left glove and shoved up his sleeve to check his enormous watch. "Another safety feature. The computer does a full systems check after a crash. It shouldn't take too long. Then we can start on our way again. A little slower this time."

The noise outside intensified. Snow and wind were slamming against the windows. Then we heard a faint crunching sound below us, too. Even through the thick soles of my boots and the rigid bottom of the sled, I could feel movement. And while I could hardly see outside, I caught enough of a glimpse through the swirls of white to notice a new problem. "Are we moving again?"

Hank laughed. "No, we're not moving, Jack. I just told you, the motor is off."

Ava gripped her seat. "No," she said, "we're definitely moving."

"We are not moving," Hank insisted.

Ava reached over and wiped the windshield with the side of her glove.

Hank's head popped forward. He looked as though he'd just seen an alien ship drop down to the ice. "Hey," he shouted, "why are we moving?!" He pulled off his other glove and drummed his fingers on his chin. "We're too light," he said. "The wind out here is too strong. And with the intake valve closed, the bottom of the craft is perfectly smooth. Our walls are catching the wind like sails." He leaned back in his seat, smiling wide. "Fascinating! I hardly expected this!"

The whole phenomenon was so terribly interesting to him that he didn't even stop to consider that there were people inside this accidental sailboat, and that he was one of them, and that, for a few minutes at least, until we could turn the motor back on, we had no way to steer. I cleared my window and looked up and out at the mountains in the distance. The Transantarctic range was to our left. We were drifting north along the invisible shore. From my pocket I removed a small compass. The needle wavered, then held in place. Our heading was just right. I grinned.

Next to me, Matt was gripping his harness, as if that would protect him. "Why are you so happy?" he asked through clenched teeth. "We're in an out-of-control vehicle in the middle of a frozen wasteland!"

I leaned back and tapped the face of the compass. "Yeah, but we're going the right way."

We sailed onward, skimming over the ice, for at least fifteen minutes before a pair of green lights sparked to life on the control panel. Hank clapped. "Good, we can start her up again."

Again I looked out at the mountains and the passing snow formations. We were going at least as fast with the wind as we had with the motor. "Or we could save the batteries and just keep sailing," I suggested.

The motor purred below us. Hank had already switched on the system. We heard another click, and without any warning, the front of the vehicle caught in the snow and held fast. The entire Snowgoer flipped, back over front, and landed on the inflatable roof. It took me a moment to realize I was hanging upside down. We all were. And all four of us had the bright idea to unbuckle at the exact same time. We tumbled into a human pile with yours truly at the bottom. Something heavy and hard pressed down on me. I couldn't breathe. The ice-encrusted sole of a boot was digging into my cheek. I tried to shout, but someone's elbow was stuffed into my mouth. Then we shifted. The human pile collapsed to the sides. I could breathe again and hear enough to notice a slight but powerful pop. Ava was shouting at Matt to get off her. Hank was apologizing. I elbowed my way up into a sitting position. The seats were above us. Yet they seemed to be getting closer. The wind was still blowing, so it was hard to notice the sound, but in all the arguing and shuffling around in the small space I heard a very real hiss. The kind of sound you hear when the air's leaking out of a beach ball.

I pointed to the collapsing roof. "That's not good, huh?"

"Out," Hank said. "Everybody out!"

We scrambled through the back of the Snowgoer, then stood and watched as the hardened sled collapsed on top of the deflating shell.

187

"What now?" Ava asked.

No one had an answer. Not Matt, not Hank. And definitely not me. Our only method of transportation lay in a depressing heap. The base was a twenty-mile walk back through the snow. An explorer named Tom Crean had nearly died attempting a similar trek. And he was legendarily tough.

If I was right, Anna was hiding out in the opposite direction, thirty miles away. So we were pretty much in the middle of nowhere. We had to either return or press on. And with the Herbie on its way, we might not survive either trip.

The landscape in front of us was a bright and terrifying desert of ice and snow. The mountains loomed to our left like angry sleeping giants. And between us and the comforts of McMurdo Station stood the same bright white cold. The wind scraped my face. We could make it part of the way back, then build a shelter to sleep the night and complete the trip in the morning.

That would be the only sane choice.

But we'd be leaving Anna behind. We'd be giving up. And I don't like giving up.

"We have to turn back," Hank said.

I protested. "But we can't just—"

"I can run," Matt said.

"What are you talking about?"

"I'm wearing the legs," Matt said.

Hank, Ava, and I all said, "What?"

"The robotic legs," he said. He knocked his gloved fist against the side of his baggy snow pants. The sound was solid. And now it made sense why he had been walking strangely. He kicked some snow at his feet. "With these I could probably run back in no time and get help."

"Wait," Ava said, "back up. Why, exactly, are you wearing the robolegs?"

Matt struggled to answer. He wouldn't look at Hank. "When we were testing the Snowgoer, I was in the Mechanical Equipment Center, and Hank had run off to get something, and the robolegs were there, and so I kind of tried them on to see how they worked, and then you came back, Hank, and I didn't want to tell you, because you kept saying to be patient, and, well, I just haven't had a chance to take them off." Slowly he looked up at his idol.

Hank's face was expressionless for a moment. Then he pointed to Matt's legs. "You've had them on all this time?"

"What?"

"You've been wearing them through all this chaos, and they're still functioning normally, even in these temperatures?"

Again Matt paused; he clearly didn't know what to say. "Y-y-yes. Yes, definitely! They're working fine." He jogged a short distance through the snow, then circled back. "They do all the work for you. And, honestly, I'm sorry I—"

"Don't worry," Hank said. "Really. Even if this isn't quite the sort of experiment I had in mind, I did bring them down here for a reason."

"So you're not disappointed in me?" Matt asked, his voice so low I could barely hear him.

"Disappointed? In you? That's absurd, Matthew. I've never been disappointed in you. You impress me daily."

189

Honestly, I think my brother may have floated above the snow for a second on the power of that compliment.

"I'm serious. I'll run back to the base," Matt said. "I could get there in—"

"No," Hank insisted. "I admire your courage, but I'm responsible for your safety, and I can't let . . ."

"You can't what?" Ava prompted him when he abruptly stopped speaking.

But Hank was looking past us, toward the base. Turning, we saw it, too. A form appeared on the horizon.

"Is that a snowmobile?" Ava asked.

"I think it might be . . ."

"You said you'd take the blame, right, Hank?" Matt asked.

"What? Me?" Hank asked. "Yes, yes. I did say that, didn't I? I will."

Moments later a snowmobile skidded to a stop some ten feet from our crumpled craft. The driver stepped off, pulled down his hood, pushed his orange-lensed goggles up on his forehead, and smiled. In a familiar Australian accent he asked, "What are you four doing all the way out here?"

# 15

# THE CALL OF THE SEALS

**A**FTER WE FINISHED CHEERING, CLAPPING, AND thanking him repeatedly, Danno squeezed Hank's shoulder. "I need to take care of the Clutterbuck judge!" he said. "Just don't forget me when you're picking the winner tomorrow."

Matt pointed back at the ice ridge. "How did you—"

Danno's mouth formed a small *o* as he breathed in slowly, then smiled with pride. "I jumped her! I happened to see you leaving the base, so I sped after you. I'd nearly caught up to you when you jumped the ramp. I figured if you four could do it in your little bubble mobile, I ought to be able to. For a split second there I did wonder if it was a bad idea, but she landed just fine."

"It's called the Snowgoer," Hank said.

"Excuse me?" Danno asked.

"It's not a bubble mobile."

"Oh, right. My apologies, mate," Danno said. "Either

way, she sure did take off with the wind. I thought I'd lost you there!"

He clapped Hank on the back, then eyed our deflated vehicle. After a quick discussion, Danno suggested we flip it over onto the shell and tow it like a sled. One of us could sit on the back of the snowmobile with him, the other three on the Snowgoer. Hank agreed, and we started working. Matt folded and tied down the deflated walls. Hank helped Danno secure the crumpled craft to the back of the snow-mobile with a pair of strong climbing ropes. Ava worked on the knots, and Matt and I gathered our emergency packs.

The cold was fierce. I stomped my feet in the snow to keep them warm, then closed my eyes and tried to dream of Tahiti, with the hot sand under my back and the sun cook-ing my chest.

192

Matt kicked a spray of snow into my face. "Are you help-ing or not?"

Danno and Hank grabbed the front of the Snowgoer and dragged it around to point in the other direction.

"Shouldn't we be going that way?" I asked, pointing toward our destination.

"No, mate, the base is behind us," Danno said.

"We can't go back to the base. We still have to find Anna," I insisted.

"That's lunacy, boy. I'm taking you all home to McMurdo."

Now, look, I'll be honest, the warmth and comfort of the station were totally appealing. We could've been back there ordering a fresh pizza. But we'd come this far, and now we had a snowmobile. Why not push on? "We have to go look for her."

"It's not safe, mate," Danno said.

"It's not that much farther," Ava added. "We know where she is."

Now Danno stopped. "You do?"

"Jack here figured it all out," Hank said. And maybe it was just the wind messing with his voice, but I'd swear I heard a hint of pride in his tone.

I looked to Ava, Matt, and Hank. "We think we know, yes." Then I pointed to the emergency packs. "It should be about thirty miles farther. We have enough supplies and food to last for a week if anything goes wrong."

"We have to do it," Ava said.

"We might as well," Matt added with a shrug.

Hank tapped the hood of the snowmobile. "We owe it to Anna to try."

Danno was shaking his head. "No! Okay? No. That's the answer. We're going back to the station."

Our Australian friend slapped Hank on the back. "Come

on now, let's not be ridiculous. We've got to get you back to judge the contest, Hank."

The Clutterbuck Prize again. In our desperate search for Anna, I hadn't been thinking about the main reason we were in Antarctica in the first place. But to Daniel Perkins the prize meant everything. His eyes were shining with intensity. His smile was oddly twisted. The combination of the two looked as fake as a plastic cactus. The more I stared, the more I saw behind those strange, glimmering eyes. All this time we'd been thinking that Franklin Golding or Evgeny Levokin might be behind the plot against Anna. But we were wrong. Anna's discovery threatened Danno more than anyone. The way her creatures sucked the salt out of water was probably far more effective than his DP-1000.

She was the roadblock on his route to a million dollars.

And he had to knock her out of the way.

"Jack, what's wrong?" Ava asked.

My stare wasn't breaking. Danno's cracked lips closed. His false smile faded.

"We have to keep going," I said.

"No, mate, we're all going back," Danno said, his breath rising in thick clouds.

"Or what? You'll leave us out here?" I waited a second before delivering the verbal uppercut. "Just like you left Anna?"

Hank spurted out, "Jack, what are you talking about?"

"You're the one who chased her out onto the ice, aren't you?" I asked.

"Come on now—"

"That does kind of make sense," Matt added. He sounded completely shocked that I'd had a good idea.

Danno said nothing.

"There's no use lying anymore. We know."

For a few long seconds no one spoke. The wind whipped around us. The storm was growing stronger by the minute, and Danno's face was as frozen as the ice beneath our boots. Then a half smile broke its way through his expressionless features. "Nobody chased her out here. She ran on her own."

"Because someone was wrecking her work," I said. "You stole her computer and her sample of the creatures."

"Listen—"

Ava jabbed a gloved finger into the air. "The honey!"

"What?" Hank asked.

"Huh?" I added.

"The sticky stuff on the counters and shelves in Anna's room," she said. "That was you, too, right? You were licking that stuff off your fingers the first time we met."

Hank winced. "That was repugnant."

"Really," Danno said, "this is ridiculous. Let's get back to the base, please."

195

Ava pointed to her pack on the edge of the sled. "I'll bet my little flying robot has some video of you going into Anna's room," she said. "He's been watching everyone."

She was bluffing; Ava hadn't even flown Fred indoors. I glanced at her pack; the drone was strapped to the outside. No one moved. The wind itself seemed to be waiting to see what Danno would do. And then he leaped across the snow, lunging for the drone. He ripped it loose, then slipped, and Fred rolled into the snow.

Danno reached down to grab it, but the drone's blades began to spin. Ava was fumbling with the old smartphone in her pocket.

Fred lifted off in a small blizzard of snow. "Stop that thing!" Danno yelled. He jumped for the robot, but it was out of reach. "Get it down here!" he yelled to Ava.

"I can't," she lied. "I think it's broken."

She was lying again.

Danno desperately hurled an ice ball at Fred and missed. "You all should've just left this whole mess alone," he barked.

"Why?" Hank asked. "Why would you steal another scientist's work?"

"The Clutterbuck Prize," Ava said. "Those creatures Anna found could make his invention irrelevant."

"This is all because of your DS-1000?" Hank asked.

"DP!" Danno shouted. "The DP-1000! How many times

do I have to tell you that? And it is not merely an invention, Dr. Weatherspoon. You may turn out a new device every three months, but the rest of us only get one shot. One good idea! And if we don't make the most of it, that's all. Well, I spent the last ten winters here in this dark, cold wasteland, working on my machine, trying to figure out every possible way to get it right. Then I found it! The DP-1000 represents ten years of work. This is my chance. I finally built a better desalination system."

"Ten percent better," Matt said. He shrugged at Hank. "That's what he said, right? I mean, I'm just saying . . . it's only ten percent."

"But it is better! Ten percent is huge! Don't you see? I improved every piece of the design, and then your friend found these little creatures that could ruin everything! I didn't want her to hide them forever. I just wanted to win the prize."

The wind conveniently calmed, as if the continent itself were pausing to listen. "And a million dollars," I added.

"Yes, yes, I wanted the money, and so I needed to get your friend Anna and her creatures out of the way. That night when she was trying to sneak off, I found her trying to steal a snowmobile. I have my own"—he nodded to his vehicle—"so I offered to drive her. I wanted to see where she'd found those things to make sure no one else could do the same. Or not for a while, at least. But on our way to the site she must have figured it out. We stopped, and she wouldn't go any farther. I tried to reason with her. I even offered her a cut of my earnings if she would wait to reveal her discovery."

Quick glares from Hank and Matt informed me that it was not appropriate to ask how much he'd offered. "But she refused," I said.

"That's right."

"So you left her out here to die."

"No, no, no, mate, you misunderstand," Danno said. He reached around to the side of his snowmobile and pulled out a gun.

I shuffled back a few steps. Hank instantly stepped in front of us and held out his arms. "Please, Mr. Perkins," Hank said. "Surely there's another solution."

"You won't win the Prize by killing the judge," Matt noted.

Danno shrugged. "And I won't win now that the judge knows I've sabotaged his friend, will I? I figure they'll find another judge. Or now that I've got the machine tuned up, I can sell it to the highest bidder."

Staring at the weapon, I remembered a detail from my reading. "Guns aren't allowed in Antarctica," I said. "That's a fake."

Danno fired a bullet into the snow.

Ava and I jumped back. "That sounded real," she said.

The ice groaned below us. Danno edged closer, aiming the gun at Hank's chest. "You see, I didn't really leave her out here to die," he said. "I left her out here to freeze. Which is exactly what I'm going to do with you. But first we're going to put a few more miles between you people and the base. Wouldn't want you to show up in the morning alive and kicking, would I? So start marching, or one of you gets a bullet."

In my twelve long years of life, I had made plenty of enemies. On the playground. In at least two foster homes. The entire poetry profession despised my siblings because we sold more copies of that one book of verse than all of theirs added together. These enemies had called me names and knocked me down. I'd been spat on once. But no one had ever threatened to shoot me. And as we started marching north, with Danno driving the snowmobile at a crawl behind us, towing our gear, I have to say I was dealing with it pretty well. Maybe the spirits of Shackleton, Scott, Amundsen, and the rest of the famous Antarctic explorers were whispering over my shoulder. Either way, I realized pretty quickly there was no point getting all weepy and scared. That wouldn't help us survive.

Danno's plan wasn't a bad one. My guess was that he'd push us as far as we could go, ditch us, then head back to the base. The blizzard would hide our tracks. He could drop our gear somewhere close to the station. It would look like we'd ventured off alone. When we were found, the rescue crew would assume we'd gotten lost in the storm. A perfectly reasonable tragedy.

Ava had her old smartphone out, pressed close to her stomach.

"What are you doing?" I asked.

"Setting Fred to follow us," she said. "He's still hovering back there, out of sight."

"Why?"

The snowmobile's engine quieted. "Cut it out!" Danno yelled. "What are you talking about up there?"

The wind roared, then calmed, and I could hear the faint pings of seals calling one another in the water below. My heart beat faster. We were miles from open water. The desert of ice stretched far out from the mountainous coast. But there were seals below us. And seals needed to breathe. Which meant there had to be holes in the ice. But where? I stopped and crouched in the snow. The ice in front of us was smooth and white in all directions.

Danno stepped off his snowmobile and stomped forward, the gun at his side. "What are you doing?" he growled.

"I need a rest," I lied. "I'm exhausted."

He pressed his foot against my back and pushed me

forward. I threw out my arms to stop myself from face-planting. "You've barely walked half a mile."

Matt took a step toward him, but Danno raised the gun. "Stay where you are, kid," he said. "And you," he added, kicking me lightly, "get up and get moving."

"Really, Mr. Perkins," Hank said, "I'm sure there's some solution that doesn't involve—"

"Move or I shoot," he shouted.

Danno returned to his snowmobile. The wind rose again, whipping up swirls of snow. We could only see fifteen or twenty feet in front of us. But that was all I needed. Just ahead I spotted the slick back of a seal as it slid down into the icy water. Ava raised her arm to point. "There's a—"

I coughed and elbowed her. "Walk around it, but whatever you do, don't stop. Just keep walking."

"What are you going to do?" Matt asked.

"I'm going to need you to use those legs."

"What are you talking about?" Hank asked.

"Just trust me," I pleaded.

"You want me to run?" Matt asked.

"No, I want you to bust open a trapdoor."

"But—"

"Just stay close," I said.

The snow was blowing so hard that the seal hole was nearly covered by the time we reached the edge of it. The slush was already beginning to harden into ice. If I didn't know it was there, I might have missed it entirely. I didn't want to give Danno any clue, so I toed right along the side, then collapsed to my knees on the other side. The ice wobbled slightly beneath me. "Pretend you're helping me up," I mumbled to Matt.

The snowmobile stopped again. I could hear Danno's footsteps pounding over the ice. "What are you doing?" he yelled.

"I can't go on," I shouted into the wind.

"We haven't even walked a mile! Get on your feet."

"He's exhausted," Matt said.

There was no point faking tears. They just would've frozen on my face. So I went with some straight-up begging. "Please! Please! Don't leave us out here to die!"

"I said, get moving!" Danno shouted again.

"I can't," I lied. "Please help me."

The crazed engineer looked frustrated and angry enough to lift me up by the back of my Big Red and hurl me the thirty miles to Anna's last dive site. Fortunately, though, he never managed to get close enough to try. He was so focused on the cowering brat who refused to go along with his murderous plan that he didn't bother to look down. "Now!" I yelled to Matt, and my brother stomped down hard with one of his partially robotic legs. His right boot broke open the ice as he desperately clambered backward, preventing himself from slipping into the water.

Danno was not so lucky. When his foot struck the newly opened trapdoor, he lost his balance and toppled forward. His eyes flashed with a mix of terror and confusion as he plunged down through the slush, falling up to his waist into the icy water. He flailed out with his arms to stop himself from going under and loosened his grip on the gun. The weapon slid across the ice.

I stood up, and for a nanosecond I believed we were free.

Then one of Danno's huge gloved hands wrapped around my ankle with the force of a boa constrictor death-gripping a helpless rat. My heels lost their grip as he yanked me down. My back slammed onto the hard-packed snow. The ice below me cracked. The water rose up out of the hole, spilling out over the snow, soaking my pants. He pulled me farther. The burning cold water wrapped around my legs.

The water was above my knees when something tightened around my arms and chest and yanked me back. I looked down. A climbing rope was wrapped around me, and the others were pulling me toward them. Hank had some lasso skills, after all, and with several great heaves I was nearly pulled clear of the seal hole. Then my progress stopped. Danno was still holding tightly to my ankle. There was no feeling left in either one of my feet, but I lifted my

203

right knee and kicked. My boot glanced off his glove. Again I was yanked backward, and this time the heel of my boot met his knuckles, and he released me with a cry of pain.

The mad inventor plunged down below his shoulders. He tried to hold himself up, but the sides of the hole were too slick with snow and slush. In all the chaos I don't know if he cried for help. As Hank and Ava propped me up onto my feet, Matt threw another line into the hole. Danno grabbed it, and my older brother dug his feet into the snow, pulling our attacker from the water.

Hank raced across the ice, grabbed the gun, then tossed it in the seal hole. "I despise those things," he said.

Ava loosened the rope they'd thrown around my chest.

Danno was shivering wildly. Slowly he sat and pulled his knees to his chest. He was soaked through, his face blue. He stuttered as he tried to speak.

"He's going to freeze to death if we don't get him warm," Hank said. He tapped Matt. "Let's get our gear."

I pulled my soaked legs up inside my oversize Big Red. Ava crouched beside me, putting her arm around my shoulders.

Hank hurried over with blankets, but Matt pulled a utility tool out of his coat and started cutting up the deflated roof and walls of the Snowgoer.

"Brilliant!" Hank said. He leaned over to me. "Wonderful

heat retention. If it were softer, it would make an amazing blanket."

First Matt handed a large square section of the shiny material to Ava, who helped me wrap myself up. Then he did the same for Danno. I can't say I was warm right away, but it blocked out the cold.

As Hank and Ava set up a stove, and Matt began digging through our packs for dry clothes, the ice began to shake. The frozen white ground rumbled like an earthquake. Was this night really going to get worse?

Two blurry yellow lights appeared in the blinding snow. There was still no feeling in my feet, so I couldn't even stand on my own. Wrapped in the remains of our inflatable vehicle, leaning on my sister, I saw the lights brighten. The rumbling intensified, and a vehicle took shape in the snow. A very large, very beautiful, and very warm-looking blue truck.

205

"Is that the Rambler?" Ava asked.

Hank waved them away from the thin ice near the seal hole. The doors on either side swung open. Britney jumped from the passenger side and raced over to me with a blanket. Levokin followed, wrapping a coat around Danno. The driver stepped out last, and even if the Rambler was her vehicle, I was more than a little surprised to see the director. She pulled at her hat and glared my way. "Everyone into the back," she ordered.

The interior was large, loud, and wonderfully warm. We stayed in place with the engine running. The heat was cranked up so high that it felt like three or four people were aiming blow-dryers at my face. Immediately Danno and I changed into dry clothes—the girls covered their eyes— while Matt removed his snow pants and unbuckled himself from the robotic legs. Warming up was somehow more painful than falling into the icy water in the first place. Then I remembered I was wearing my self-drying underpants. I pressed the button on the waistband, and a blast of wonderfully warm air rushed through the fabric. The skin of my lower legs burned, so I kept the boxers running for added warmth. I decided I'd have to talk to Hank about making an entire line of such clothes. Pants, for example, would have been nice. I'd forgotten to pack spares, so Ava offered me the Hello Kitty sweats she despised. They were pink and covered with tiny cat faces, and I did not care in the slightest.

We still hadn't started driving yet, and the director and Hank rotated the front seats around to face the rest of us on our bench seats in the back. Danno, Levokin, and Matt on one side, Ava, Britney, and I on the other. Britney put her arm around me, and I was so cold that I didn't even bother to check to see if Matt was jealous.

Levokin poured a few cups of hot chocolate from a thermos, and Ava and Matt told our story. The Australian sat quietly shivering through it all, avoiding the director's cold stare as Levokin forced him to drink. At one point, she leaped out of her seat and charged at Danno. She lifted the back of her hand as if she was going to strike him, then stopped and punched the roof of her beloved vehicle. "Ten winters! I should've known you'd lose your mind." She turned to us and tapped the side of her head. "No one can stay sane when they winter-over ten years in a row. The darkness gets to you. All those months without sunlight. I never should've let him stay here for ten winters."

"I'm . . . I'm s-s-sorry," Danno said.

"Too late," she spat back. "I don't even know what to do with you. We don't really have a court system here."

After a long pause, I raised my hand. Holding my own mug of hot chocolate just below my mouth, struggling to get the words past my chattering teeth, I asked, "Wh-wh-what made you come after us?"

"Sophie told me about your plan after the first round of the karaoke contest," Britney said. "She was worried. And so was I. Two days of Happy Camper training doesn't exactly make you Ernest Shackleton. Why didn't you guys tell me what you were up to? Didn't you trust me?"

"You would have tried to stop us," Ava said.

Britney shrugged. "Good point. You're right."

"So you decided to come get us?" Matt asked.

207

Britney nodded to the driver. "First I had to tell the director, since we needed the Rambler to get out here quickly."

The director squinted menacingly at Hank. "I had to plow straight through that ice ridge. If there is so much as a scratch on my baby, you're covering the damages."

"Then we recruited Evgeny," Britney added. "By that point it was clear he was going to whip Golding, anyway."

"Really?" Ava asked. "You won?"

"No, I leave early," the Russian said. "I already prove I am best thanks to the Billy Joel. Every time. In my home they call me the Karelin of Karaoke."

"Huh?" I said.

"Karelin was an amazing Olympic wrestler," Ava said.

I didn't bother asking how she knew that.

Hank jutted out his chin and massaged his throat. "Next time I might like to challenge you, Mr. Levokin. I've been compared to Sinatra on occasion."

This was light-years from true. Matt shook his head my way, silently suggesting I ignore the boast. "How'd you know where we were?" Matt asked. "You could've driven right past us. Or even in another direction altogether."

"That would be your sister's doing," Britney said.

"What did you do?" I asked Ava.

Ava made a clicking noise with her tongue. "I wanted

to make sure they knew where we were, in case they didn't hear from us. So last night I kind of wrote a little program that allows you to track Fred's location from a laptop, and I showed Sophie how to use it."

"Kind of?"

"That's why you had him with us," Hank said, smiling proudly.

"And why you set him to follow us once he went airborne," I added.

"Stupid robot," Danno said.

"Quiet!" Levokin shouted at him.

"You sound better already, Mr. Perkins," the director added. "Warming up, are we?"

He sneered and said nothing.

The director turned to Ava. "I'm impressed, young lady," she said. "We might never have found you otherwise."

Ava was watching Hank. "It's not that I didn't trust you to get us there and back safely . . ."

He laughed and shook his head. "What? Oh, no, please. Don't worry about that for a second. I wouldn't trust me, either." He peered out the window at the distant mountains, then eyed Danno, wrapped up and shivering. "I'm not really suited for this kind of adventuring, anyway. It's far too intense."

Britney laughed, but the director's face was blank.

"What about you?" I asked the director. "I thought you would've been happy to get rid of us."

She huffed. "Believe me, young man, I would love nothing more than for you to disappear from McMurdo. But I don't want to get rid of you by losing you out on the ice. That might cost me my job. I want to see you safely onto a plane home." She stared at each of us in turn, then lingered on Hank. "What? Did you expect something warm and fuzzy? You're not going to get it. Not from me. This station is for scientific research. Not intellectual tourism and silly prizes from a sock manufacturer." She eyed Danno again. "And it is certainly no place for thieves and saboteurs."

"Do not speak poorly of Mr. Clutterbuck," Levokin said. He reached down and snapped the top of his socks—the same pair he'd been wearing two days before. "Almost seventeen days. This man is genius."

"What are you going to do with Perkins?" Britney asked the director.

"We'll figure it out back at the base," she said. "Evgeny, do you think Mr. Perkins is now well enough to travel? No signs of hypothermia?"

Levokin placed the back of his hand against Danno's forehead, checked his pulse, then elbowed him in the shoulder. "He is fine. You worry too much about cold water. In Russia, we do these plunges for health."

"Good," the director replied. "Then would you mind tying Mr. Perkins to the back of the snowmobile? At least a dozen knots, please. Bind him like luggage, and make sure that silly inflatable vehicle is securely strapped to the back, as well. We don't want to leave that out here. That would be littering."

"Will be my pleasure," the Russian answered, grabbing Danno out of his seat.

"It's not silly," Hank said under his breath.

The director started to follow Levokin and Danno outside. "Good luck to the rest of you."

"Wait," Ava said. "What do you mean? Aren't we all going back to the base?"

"McMurdo? Of course not," the director answered. "I'll take Mr. Perkins back to the base on the snowmobile. We can determine what to do with him there. Evgeny will join you when he's finished with his chore here, and I trust he will keep you safe."

"Safe from what?" I asked.

"You have a long trip ahead of you," the director said. "You've come all this way already. You might as well go rescue your friend."

# 16
# WORLD OF WONDERS

**M**Y BROTHER HAD JUST SPENT THE LAST FEW days in a scientific paradise meeting with some of the brightest minds in the world. He had solved a biological puzzle that had stumped Hank—figuring out the importance of Anna's creatures. He'd road-tested a pair of mechanical legs, without their inventor's permission, and quite possibly saved all our lives. But the highlight of his time at the South Pole may have been driving the Rambler. Once the director was gone, Hank declared that he didn't feel like taking the wheel, and Matt begged the others to let him drive. Now, as we plowed through the snow, he leaned so far forward, he nearly had his forehead pressed against the windshield, and his smile looked like it might be permanent.

The worst of the storm struck an hour after we watched Danno and the director ride away, leaving a miniature blizzard in their wake. The wind tore down from the

Transantarctic Mountains, slamming the side of the Rambler like some angry old mountain god trying to knock us onto our side. Yet the vehicle kept slowly grinding onward—warm, loud, and beautifully dry. The weather was not going to stop us, and since we'd grabbed our supplies and equipment from the Snowgoer and stashed them in the back, we were prepared for just about anything.

The warmth was slowly seeping through me. My feet and ankles were still burning from the cold, but I could feel the Rambler's tracked wheels crunching over the snow below through the thick fleece socks Ava had lent me. Both she and Levokin had nodded off to sleep. Hank sat beside our young driver, and Britney was leaning forward from her spot in the back, watching Matt carefully. As the Rambler rolled over the ice, I couldn't help thinking about the world below. How strange that there was water beneath us! And not just any water, but a sea stocked with vibrant, weird, and wild forms of life. Crablike creatures and starfish and huge, fat, slick seals were darting and kicking and playing around in that frigid and hidden world. Trillions of tiny shrimplike krill. Anna Donatelli had found her amazing creatures in that icy darkness. What other undiscovered life-forms might be lurking down there?

Several hours later the vehicle stopped shaking and rattling from the wind. I'd gotten so used to the noise that it

took me a few minutes to realize it had stopped. The worst
of the storm was over, and the sky was transforming slowly
into a brighter blue canopy. This was Antarctica's version
of dawn, and the timing could not have been more perfect.
The others in the back were still sleeping, but I was staring out the half-defrosted windshield. Matt pointed into the
distance. A lone woman
stood waving.

She wore a Big Red.
The air was far below
freezing, and yet she was,
standing out there on
the ice, with the moun-

tains rising high behind her, and her short blond hair was
bright in the sun. After those first few waves of her arms, she
stood with her hands on her hips, waiting. Hank rubbed his
eyes with his gloves, then clapped. I elbowed Ava.

"That's her, right?" Matt asked Hank.

"That's her!"

Levokin unbuckled his harness and crawled forward for
a closer look. "Is she okay?"

"Anna? She looks fine!" Hank exclaimed.

"No, not Anna," Levokin said. "My wet suit. Can you
see her?"

Anna's camp slowly came into focus. The shelter behind

214

her was tall and wide enough to drive a minivan through the middle. From our position, I couldn't tell how far it stretched back, but it looked enormous. It had taken five of us to build our tiny fort during Happy Camper training. How in the world had she constructed that beauty all on her own?

"My hab!" Hank yelled.

"Your what?"

"My self-inflating habitat. Another one of the items I'd sent down here ahead of time." He caught Levokin's confused stare and explained. "It's designed for space missions. Landing on the Moon or Mars. The same technology as the Snowgoer, only instead of a vehicle, it blows up into the walls and ceiling of a rather roomy living space. I thought this would be the perfect place for a test. Anna must have borrowed it."

"Yes, like she 'borrowed' my wet suit," Levokin grumbled. "Where I come from, this is called stealing."

When the Rambler finally rolled to a stop in front of her camp, Hank jumped out and rushed to Anna, but she dodged his attempted hug and climbed into the back of the vehicle before we even had a chance to get out. "What have you got to eat?" she demanded.

Matt pointed to one of the bags.

Anna started digging through the wrong pack, so Ava tossed her an energy bar. The scientist grabbed it, tore off a chunk with her teeth, and chomped with a wide-open mouth. Her eyes closed. Her face relaxed. "Thank you." As she grabbed a candy bar and flopped down into a seat, Hank joined us in the back. "I ran out of food yesterday," she said. "What took you so long?"

He patted her affectionately on both shoulders. "How's my hab?"

Our mentor was so excited that Anna's open-mouthed chewing didn't even bother him. "Phobos?" I mouthed to Ava. She smiled.

"The habitat? Spacious, warm, altogether pleasant," she said. Her cheeks were full and red, and she was larger than I'd expected. She had the build of an ultimate fighter, a slightly husky voice, and a strong accent. "You don't mind that I used it, do you, Henry?"

"Of course not," he said. "All in the service of science. Congratulations on your discovery. Those creatures are a true marvel."

She leaned around Hank and held up her hands in the direction of the Russian. "Evgeny, your wet suit is in perfect working order, and I hereby swear"—she placed her hand on her chest—"that I will not borrow it again without telling you."

"You say this last time."

Dropping her hand, she frowned and glanced up at the sky. "Yes, right, I did, didn't I? Well, then, you know that my vows aren't worth much. So I'd advise you to keep a closer watch over your inventions. That's good advice for you, too, young lady," she said, pointing to Ava. "I hear you have a bright future. Men are often threatened by intelligent women, as they should be, and I assure you, they'll do whatever they can to slow you down. You have to keep pushing, pushing, pushing!" She glanced around. "You know it was that Australian who sabotaged me, yes?"

Ava's mouth hung open slightly, and Matt was equally flabbergasted. This woman switched subjects like they were TV channels.

"Yes. It's a long story," Britney said. "The director and Danno were actually with us, but she took him back to the base."

"After he tried to leave us for dead," Ava added.

"Yes, well, he certainly surprised me. Those long winters do fry the brain, though. That is why most people go home for at least a few months. I wonder what they'll do with him back at McMurdo." She didn't wait for an answer; something like a smile formed on her face. "Now, you three . . . you are Ava, obviously. You're Jack," she said, pointing to me, "the one who writes Hank's e-mails, and I suppose that makes you Matthew."

After all he'd done, I felt bad. "Sometimes he prefers Matt," I said.

"Matthew is fine," my brother said. Staring at Anna, he mumbled, "You're b-b-beautiful." Then he closed his eyes, clenched his teeth, and tried again. "Your research, I mean. Your research is beautiful."

"Wait, how do you know I write his e-mails?" I asked.

"Punctuation," she said. "Hank's is perfect. He's quite the grammarian. Lately his messages have displayed the careless affectations of an iPhone-addicted tween. Be careful, young man. Following the rules of writing is good for your brain. You should consider the rules of fashion, too."

My pants. I'd forgotten all about the Hello Kitty sweats. That one burned a little. "I'll work on my wardrobe if you go easier on the exclamation points."

"Touché!" she replied. She stood and started out of the vehicle. "Let's get inside the hab. There is much to see."

Levokin hurried into the habitat first, and Hank and Anna followed, firing questions as if it were some kind of competition. Matt was barely a half step behind them, trying to catch every word.

Inside, all I could manage was a simple, dumbfounded "Wow."

"Seriously," Ava said.

The inflated walls and roof created a lofty space lined with solar-powered lights, and Anna had shaped beds, couches, and even a kind of dining nook out of snow. A

central mound with a flattened top served as a table, with a semicircular ice bench around it. She'd even carved designs into the snow, resembling etching vines and trees. Anna caught me staring at her handiwork. "I set up the inflatable and some of the equipment during my last visit, and there is a lot of downtime when you're all alone out here, so I did a little extra work," she said. "Plus I knew you'd all arrive eventually, so I wanted the place to look nice. You got the Verne reference, Henry?"

"No, he did," Ava said, pointing to me.

Anna's eyebrows creased downward. "How?"

I told her about discovering the interview in the magazine. If she was impressed with my detective work, she didn't show it, but she was absolutely delighted that one of Hank's minions, as she called us, had solved her puzzle before him. "What did you think I meant by my first love?" she asked him.

Hank blushed. One of us laughed. Okay, it was me, and lasers practically shot out of Hank's eyes. With great effort I kept my mouth closed, stifling a smile. "Nothing, nothing," Hank said. He walked over and kneeled before a large hole she'd carved into the ice floor. "This is your access point?"

"Yes, that's it," she said. "It's a constant fight to keep it open for my dives, especially since all I had was a pickax and a snow saw. One night a seal popped through and tried to get into my sleeping bag. If you hadn't arrived today, I might have had to invite him back for dinner."

Standing in a far corner, inspecting the seams of his precious wet suit, Levokin muttered something in Russian. "Seals! Often they are in my nightmares, playing cards in basement of my mother's house, barking. Always with the barking."

No one spoke; some stories are better off ignored.

"I still can't believe you swim in there," Ava said.

"I'd suggest you try it yourself, but at your age, you'd probably go into shock," Anna said. "That would be unfortunate."

"Have you found more of the creatures?" Matt asked.

"What kind of question is that?" she fired back.

Matt's face paled, as if she'd punched him in the stomach.

Anna pulled a plastic tarp off one of the walls, revealing six clear containers filled with water and the wriggling, mucus-like creatures. "Thanks to this lovely hab, I was nearly able to set up a proper laboratory. I have thirty-seven creatures here at the moment, but there is an enormous population down on the bottom. These alone are producing far more water than I can use." She watched them in silence, then turned and crouched before the hole. "I wish I could show you all what it's like down there," Anna said. "It's a true world of wonders."

I nudged Ava. "Do it."

"No," she whispered.

Matt whispered, "Come on."

"No," she replied, a little louder.

"What?" Anna asked. "Tell me."

Ava shifted her jaw to one side. She stared at the roof as she replied. "Well, I kind of . . . I built something and brought it down here to test, but it's probably not . . ."

"She brought a submarine," I said.

Anna brightened. "Perfect! Let's take her for a swim, then, shall we? She captures video?"

Ava nodded nervously.

"Then let's see what she can find."

After my sister went outside to grab Shelly from the Rambler, then returned to get her submersible ready, Levokin lay down his wet suit and watched. "This is very nice work! You built this?"

"She did," Hank said with pride, "and I get goose bumps thinking about what she'll be capable of in five years' time."

Ava opened her laptop and set it on a blanket. She plugged an Xbox controller into the computer.

"Seriously?" I said. "You took the other one?"

She apologized, shrugged, and ran another set of cables from the laptop to the submarine. Then she clamped one of the submarine's panels shut and spun the rear propeller. "She can run on her own, too, without the cables, but

I think we're better off this way, so we can control her and watch the live feed."

"What's her maximum depth?" Anna asked.

"About fifty meters."

"Perfect. It's no deeper than twenty here. She'll be fine."

The Russian lightly rapped his knuckles against the aluminum hull. "This submarine is girl?" he asked.

"Her name is Shelly," I said.

"Beautiful. Beautiful."

With Anna's help, my sister lowered the craft into the water. Moments later, a live feed from Shelly's camera appeared on Ava's screen. The scene was similar to what we'd pulled off the memory card from Anna's headcam, only the resolution was incredibly clear. Spires of bluish white ice rose up from the bottom. The water was thick with translucent plankton and krill. The shadow of a seal passed over the submarine.

"Take her lower," Anna suggested.

Without hesitation Ava steered Shelly closer to the seafloor. Soon we could see the yellowish creatures crawling through and across the grayish mud, and the tiny chunks of pure, freshwater ice floating up toward the surface. Hank gasped. Matt actually used the word "marvelous," like he was suddenly English. And, believe me, I understood that this was a serious moment. Those weird little creatures had the potential to save millions of lives. I got that. Totally. But as I watched those little ice cubes drift upward, I couldn't help thinking about where they'd come from.

"Seriously?" Matt said. "You're laughing?"

I shrugged. Funny is funny.

"Amazing, isn't it?" Anna said. Then she grabbed Hank by the shoulder. "So, what do you think? Is this a million-dollar discovery?"

"Well, I've looked over the other proposals, and I wasn't terribly impressed with any of them, but you didn't formally enter the contest, and I'm not—"

"I entered."

"No, you didn't."

"Sure, I did," she said, pointing at Levokin. "Under his name."

"My name?" Levokin asked.

"That's the least I could do," she said. "Without your wet suit, I never would have found these guys. So if anyone should get the money, it's you. What do you think, Henry?"

"Well, unless the judge is perfectly insane," Hank said, "I suspect you will emerge victorious."

The Russian wrapped Anna in a crushing embrace, swinging her around twice before dropping her back to her feet. She was as stiff as a totem pole. Then she brushed off her jacket as if the hug had somehow dirtied her clothes.

Levokin's laugh was so loud that it threatened to collapse the entire habitat. A few days earlier, I might've said the singing, violin-playing, wet-suit-inventing Russian was the oddest creature down at the bottom of the world. The F. E. might have received a vote, too. Maybe Victor Valenza. But this strong and brilliant woman wiping the affection off her shirtsleeves had to be the strangest of all. She'd bolted into the frozen wilderness to protect a discovery, risking her life for the sake of science. But what she'd just done there in her makeshift lab catapulted her to a whole new level of crazy. She was about to give away a million dollars.

And don't tell the others, but that made me admire her all the more.

# 17

# THE FUTURE OF ENERGY

**KAY. SOME NEWS. BUT FIRST LET ME CATCH YOU UP**
on what happened down in Antarctica. After staying in Anna's surprisingly comfortable temporary
habitat, we survived the trip back to McMurdo
Station, arriving in plenty of time for the Clutterbuck Prize.

By that point, Danno was already gone. The director had
him flown out to an old station in the middle of the Antarctic continent with enough supplies to last him a month.
The spot was so remote, he wouldn't even be able to find any
penguins to talk to, let alone people, and she figured this
would be a fitting punishment until she decided what to
do with him. As for the Prize, Anna Donatelli and Evgeny
Levokin won as expected, and dozens of scientists crowded
around the tank full of creatures, eager to drink the delicious
water. And, yes, I laughed every time someone remarked on
the taste. Go ahead, call me juvenile.

The real fun started when J. F. Clutterbuck joined us via

satellite video, appearing on a large screen to congratulate the winner. Levokin was so excited, he pulled off his boots and waved his socks in front of the camera, urging the billionaire to smell them. This wasn't possible, of course, but the rest of us certainly did catch the odor, and it was pungently obvious that the stink-fighting power of the material had long since faded. Victor Valenza fainted. Others coughed and pressed their woolen hats to their noses. And when Clutterbuck realized what was happening, he was completely dismayed. He demanded that Hank collect the socks and send them to his research headquarters for analysis. Then he decided he wanted Levokin flown in along with them, to have his feet tested. From that point the evening generally crumbled into chaos.

After a few more days at McMurdo and then four endless flights, we arrived back in Brooklyn. Was it good to get home? I don't know. My room is larger than the space I shared with my siblings down in Antarctica, but somehow it feels smaller. And the whole world seems different, too. Everything is a tiny bit duller, as if the city had been retinted in some kind of photo-editing app. The sky just isn't the same, either; it just doesn't feel as grand or cosmic. At the moment, I'm at my desk, scribbling all this down so I don't forget anything we've just been through. Maybe it's a way to relive the experience, too, and make sure the bottom of the world remains alive in my brain. But I'll admit, it's kind of hard to concentrate. Why? Well, Hank and Min just left, and we've had an exciting development.

Let me back up again. Three days ago, when we returned to our apartment, Min was already waiting at the door. Bags loaded with groceries and takeout were piled around her feet. She practically tackled us when we got out of the wide black sedan, and I'd never seen her smile so genuinely. We plowed through all the food, slept forever, then woke to find that Min had brought us more provisions. Soups and cookies and breads, still warm from the oven, that tasted like cake. She must have visited us five times that first day and six or seven the next. This morning, she was once again packing our fridge with goodies and stocking our cabinets with vitamins when Hank burst through the door. We hadn't seen him since our return. His face was red. There were deep, dark circles under his eyes and dark blotches on his chin. His fingers were stained with Sharpie ink. When he saw Min, he stopped. "You," he said.

"Me," she replied. "What's wrong?"

"Wrong?" he asked. His eyes scanned the floor, then the ceiling. Anything to avoid her gaze. "Nothing! Not really, anyway."

He grabbed the vitamins and tossed them back to her.

"Please," he said. "These are useless. All they do is produce expensive and colorful . . . never mind."

Ava and Matt had come out of their rooms. I was leaning against the wall, watching. "What's going on, Hank?" my brother asked.

Now Hank stared at Min.

"What?" she asked.

"Well, you see, I can't really say too much . . . secrets and things of that sort . . . but an associate of mine has run into a little problem with one of her business ventures . . . A big problem, really. Massive. The future of energy could very well be at stake."

"And?" Ava asked.

"Well, the three of you proved surprisingly useful down at McMurdo. Ava, I was amazed. Matt, you astounded me." My brother looked happy enough to cry. "Even you were helpful, Jack." He stopped. Maybe he saw my reaction. Or maybe he just realized his mistake on his own. Either way, he corrected himself. "No, especially you, Jack. And, well, I'm wondering if you three wouldn't mind coming out to Hawaii to . . . well . . . help me?"

While Min explained to Hank that this was completely irresponsible and that there was no way she was going to let us fly off to Hawaii after we'd just gotten home from

Antarctica, my chest swelled with pride. Matt, Ava, and I looked at one another, and in that silence we said everything. We'd never been to Hawaii, and another trip with Hank sounded a lot more interesting than sitting around our apartment. So we split up, returned to our rooms, and started to pack.

# THIS IS REALITY, PEOPLE!

**O**NE OF THE MAIN RULES OF *BILL NYE THE SCIENCE GUY* was that the show had to focus on real science and technology. No jetpacks or teleporters. We decided to use the same approach with *Jack and the Geniuses*. So even though some of the inventions and devices might seem a little weird or wild, they are based in reality. Here are a few of our favorites.

**SLIPPERY WINDOWS:** Remember when Jack loses his grip while trying to climb up to the balcony? The material that causes him to fall is based on a substance called SLIPS, which was invented by a Harvard University chemist named Joanna Aizenberg. Her inspiration was the slick stuff the pitcher plant uses to force flies to slide down into its trap. She has envisioned a range of possible uses, including permanently nonstick surfaces or coatings that could prevent ice from building up on airplane wings.

**FRED:** We're sure you've seen a drone or two. Maybe you're lucky enough to have one yourself. Our inspiration for Fred is AirDog, a flying robot that captures video and can follow a mountain biker pedaling full speed by tracking the Wi-Fi signal in the rider's smartphone. This should remind you of a scene in the book . . . we just don't want to say which one in case you're cheating and reading this part first!

**SHELLY:** A kid building her own submarine—impossible, right? Not exactly. A seventeen-year-old named Justin Beckerman constructed his own submersible in the basement of his parents' home using mostly spare parts. And his parents actually let him test the submarine in the lake behind their house, too—with Justin inside! He dove ten feet and cruised near the bottom for thirty minutes. And no, it did not leak.

**HUMAN CATAPULTS:** Genius is applied in some of the strangest ways, and this is one such example. First of all, human catapults really do exist. But they are purely for thrills. Our favorite version was developed by a mechanical engineer to launch people into lakes and other large bodies of water. Up onto buildings? Not yet. But maybe Hank will get that working eventually.

**SELF-DRIVING CARS:** You'll probably be riding in one of these when you're older. The cars are basically robots packed with cameras, radars, and other sensors that collect loads of information about their surroundings. Advanced computer programs churn through all this data and, among other things, decide whether it's safe for the car to keep cruising or if it should stop (or swerve) to avoid a collision. And yes, we both want one.

**ROBOLEGS:** Technically these are known as exoskeletons. Think of them as motorized suits. Some encase a person's entire body, while others cover only their legs or arms. In each instance, the motors and metal in the robotic armor do the work of our muscles and bones. Today, engineers are developing robotic legs that will help soldiers carry heavy packs over long distances without getting tired and will allow certain wheelchair-bound individuals to walk upright. The most famous exoskeleton is the Iron Man suit . . . but that high-flying, laser-firing model may just be impossible.

**SNOWGOING:** While a snowblowing vehicle might not be able to achieve the same speeds as Hank's invention, the flexible, inflatable material he uses is inspired by reality. For more than a decade, scientists have been developing materials that could eventually form the walls of inflatable space habitats. These materials would have to be tough enough to withstand strikes from the debris that circles Earth. The bits and pieces of broken satellites and abandoned stations known as space junk travel so fast that even a pebble-sized fragment can punch a hole in the wall of a spacecraft.

# TEN ABSOLUTELY ESSENTIAL QUESTIONS ABOUT ANTARCTICA

**NTARCTICA IS A STRANGE AND FANTASTIC PLACE,** and not only because it's covered in ice. There are also some unusual rules in this continent at the bottom of the world.

When humans find new territory, we tend to fight over it. Even though Antarctica is one of the coldest, driest, and windiest places on Earth, we started to do just that down at the South Pole. So in 1959, a group of nations signed the Antarctic Treaty, which established the continent as a scientific preserve. Basically, everyone agreed not to conduct any business or military activity down there, and to focus strictly on research. That's one of the reasons Hank calls it "a scientific paradise." There have been more treaties since then, and in a loose kind of way, different nations are laying claim to certain territories by setting up bases. The United States base at McMurdo Station, where our story is set, is one such example.

## TEN ABSOLUTELY ESSENTIAL QUESTIONS ABOUT ANTARCTICA

We hope this book inspires you to do some research of your own on this fabulous portion of our planet. Once you start learning about the South Pole, you'll probably have about a thousand questions. So we thought we would address the most important ones first.

**I. DO THEY REALLY HAVE GOOD PIZZA?** Yes! In the past, the kitchen at McMurdo Station served meals only four times a day. But scientists keep strange hours. Sometimes they work out in the field for twenty-four hours, and then get back to the base at four o'clock in the morning, completely famished. So, to help out the scientists, the base changed its rules and introduced twenty-four-hour pizza. They even have those nice insulated bags to keep the slices warm while the scientists travel out onto the ice. And the researchers we spoke with swear that the pizza's just as good cold.

**2. HOW IS IT DARK TWENTY-FOUR HOURS A DAY IN THE WINTER?** That's a tricky one. If you were to draw a line between the North Pole and the South Pole, straight through the center of Earth, that line would be the planet's axis. Every day, Earth completes one full turn around this axis. As a result of this turn, we have night and day. The South Pole is covered in darkness part of the year because Earth is tilted slightly. During the summer, the planet's bottom section, right around the tip of the axis, is constantly facing the sun. So even when Earth completes a full spin, the South Pole never turns away from those rays. In the winter, as the planet moves along its annual track around the sun, the bottom of the world is tilted away from the light. So for those few months, the South Pole is trapped in darkness. And it's cold. And windy. And totally brutal.

### 3. WHAT HAPPENS TO A COMPASS AT THE SOUTH POLE?

First of all, there are actually two poles: the geographic one and the magnetic one. The geographic South Pole is the very bottom of that axis we just discussed. If this imaginary axis were, say, a very large broom handle running through the middle of the planet, then the broom would pop out the bottom at the geographic South Pole. The top would stick out at the North Pole. And Earth would spin around the handle. But here's where things get a little tricky. The inside, or core, of Earth is largely made of iron, which churns as Earth turns, creating a magnetic field. That's why compasses work. The needle in a compass lines up with that magnetic field. But the spinning iron also sloshes a little inside Earth. Because of this slow sloshing, the magnetic field does not quite align with Earth's spin axis, and so the magnetic poles end up in different spots than the geographic poles. Also, at the magnetic South Pole, the field lines aren't quite going north. You can imagine them rising up out of the planet instead. Then they start curving and heading north. So at the exact magnetic pole, a standard compass would not

238

work effectively. But at the geographic South Pole, or any-where else in Antarctica, a standard compass would still reveal north, south, east, and west. That's why Jack is able to use his compass as the group cruises over the ice in chapter 14. He and the geniuses are still far away from the precise magnetic South Pole.

**4. DO THEY ACTUALLY SUGGEST PACKING CANDY?** Ah, right, back to the important matters. Yes, they really do rec-ommend that researchers bring candy out into the field with them. Scientists burn a great many calories while working on the ice, and candy—or sugar—is one of the ways they quickly restore their energy reserves. Apparently it's not always very good, though. McMurdo often gets shipments of expired treats that nobody else wants.

**5. HOW CAN YOU GET DEHYDRATED WITH ALL THE SNOW AROUND?** Yes, that's a weird one. But even though the scien-tists are surrounded by frozen water, much of Antarctica is actually desert. The air is so dry it sucks the moisture right out of your body, and visitors often complain of chapped skin.

**6. DID THE ORIGINAL EXPLORERS EAT PUPPIES?** Dogs, penguins, seals—they ate anything that would allow them to survive. They definitely didn't have twenty-four-hour pizza.

**7. IS ANTARCTICA MELTING?** The enormous sheets of ice that surround the continent melt and refreeze each year.

Some scientists worry that climate change could force these ice sheets to melt even faster and cause big problems. The West Antarctic ice sheet, for example, is bigger than Mexico, and if that chunk of ice were to fall into the Southern Ocean, sea levels across the world could rise, causing serious damage to coastal cities.

**8. DO SCIENTISTS REALLY LOOK FOR CREATURES UNDER THE ICE?** Yes, definitely. While we don't know of any marine life-forms that can convert saltwater into freshwater like the creatures in our story, scientists are always searching for new species in the dark, cold waters below the ice. One of our favorites is the sea pig, which is four to six inches long and looks like a cross between an empanada and a terribly swollen, twenty-toed foot. Strangely enough, it is also a member of the sea cucumber family.

**9. WHAT DOES ANTARCTICA HAVE TO DO WITH OTHER PLANETS?** The Dry Valleys in the mountains near McMurdo Station are, well, extremely dry, and often covered with gravel instead of snow. The conditions are somewhat similar to Mars, so researchers have tested equipment in the Dry Valleys that they hope to use one day on the Red Planet. Scientists who study Europa—one of Jupiter's moons—also travel to Antarctica for research. An enormous sheet of ice covers Europa, but underneath that ice lies a deep ocean that could be teeming with life. Scientists hope that by studying the ice-covered seas around Antarctica, they may be able to learn more about that distant moon. Plus it's a much shorter flight.

**10. DO PEOPLE SWIM IN THE WATERS OF ANTARCTICA?**
Yes, but only the brave ones.

# THE DENSITY DIFFERENCE

## BY BILL NYE

**O**NE OF THE KEY IDEAS IN OUR STORY REVOLVES around density, or the number of particles of a material packed into a given amount of space. The plot hinges on the density difference between frozen water and liquid water, and between saltwater and freshwater. For the first two, you conduct a density experiment every time you pop an ice cube into a glass of water. The ice cube floats, right? This happens because there are fewer particles of water packed into that little cube than there would be in a cube of liquid water of the same size. That means the ice is less dense than the surrounding water in the glass, and as a result, it floats.

To see the density difference between saltwater and freshwater, here is a famous experiment that you can carry out at home—without putting anyone in danger.

## MATERIALS

A glass baking dish
Tap water
A measuring spoon
1 tablespoon of salt
A glass of tap water
Food coloring

## STEPS

1. Fill a glass baking dish halfway with freshwater. Tap water is fine.
2. Put 1 tablespoon of salt into the glass of tap water and stir it well. Add a little extra salt if you're feeling lucky.
3. Add a dash of food coloring to the glass of salted water. I like blue.
4. Now slowly pour the salty water into the dish. Slowly, please!

The salty blue water sinks to the bottom, and stays sunk. You can see the density difference for yourself. Thus saltwater is denser than freshwater. This is not just a fun fact; it is critical to the health of the world's oceans, which are made of both freshwater and saltwater. The sinking saltwater helps drive circulation within the ocean, and powers underwater currents as well. Some scientists call this movement of saltwater and freshwater the ocean's conveyor belt, because it moves around so much heat and so many materials.

# ACKNOWLEDGMENTS

As a kid, I was greatly influenced by Edward Stratemeyer, who created the fictional Tom Swift, which led to the life of the equally fictional Tom Swift Jr. By means of various writers, Tom Swift Jr. and his buddy Bud Barclay used science to create technologies that seemed out of reach, but still reasonable. Although I could only imagine flying labs, diving seacopters, and outposts in space, the thing was, I really could imagine them. My dad called himself Ned Nye, Boy Scientist, as a means to inspire us I guess. My mom was a remarkable puzzle solver and was recruited to work on the notorious Enigma code during the Second World War. She believed girls could do just about anything. Like many young aspiring scientists, I had fantastic teachers: Mrs. McGonagle, Mr. Lawrence, Ms. Hrushka, Mr. Morse, and especially Mr. Lang. He got me enthralled with physics and engineering.

I very much want you to have a chance to imagine your own remarkable futures. I want to give you a chance to explore and address world-sized problems—let's call them opportunities. I want you to read books. This task was beyond me. But then I met Greg Mone. He is the genius behind Jack et al. Greg took my rudimentary ideas and made them into something wonderful. Greg and I hope you enjoy these adventures. We hope they give you an idea or two so that you can go out there and change the world. —BILL NYE

Nika, Clare, Eleanor, Dylan. Mathias and Maureen. Don, Treat Yourself Nails, and Nina, for workspace. Pops, who would've loved this one. Scottish. Pie in the Sky. BtB. Jet, for logic. Nasuni. Dr. Schmidt, for amazing anecdotes. Janet Zade and all my school supporters. Haney, Cantor and Mosher at PopSci, for YBW?! Marc and Nick. Jen Carlson. Howard Reeves and the amazing Abrams crew. And of course, Mr. Nye! Thank you all. **—GREGORY MONE**

# ABOUT THE AUTHORS

**BILL NYE** IS A SCIENCE EDUCATOR, mechanical engineer, television host, and *New York Times* bestselling author with a mission: to help foster a scientifically literate society and help people everywhere understand and appreciate the science that makes our world work. Nye is best known for his Emmy award-winning children's show, *Bill Nye the Science Guy*, and for his new Netflix series, *Bill Nye Saves the World*. As a trusted science educator, Nye has appeared on numerous television programs, including *Good Morning America*, *CNN New Day*, *Late Night with Seth Meyers*, *Last Week Tonight with John Oliver*, and *Real Time with Bill Maher*. He currently splits his time between New York City and Los Angeles. Follow him online at www.billnye.com

**GREGORY MONE** IS A NOVELIST and science journalist who has written several books for children, including *Fish* and *Dangerous Waters: An Adventure on the Titanic*. He lives on Martha's Vineyard, in Massachusetts. Follow him online at www.gregorymone.com.

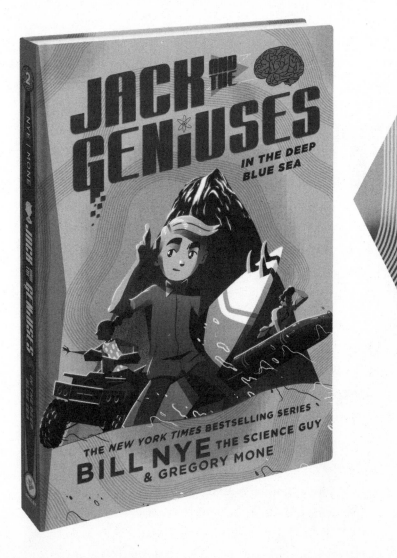

# 1

# INSIDE THE UNDERPLANE

**T**HE CLIFFS OF NIHOA ISLAND STOOD TALL AS WE soared above the calm blue water. *Nihoa* means "toothed" in Hawaiian, but the jagged mass of gray-green rock jutting up out of the Pacific Ocean looked like the rotten molar of a sea monster. We were flying low in a small six-seater airplane, and I really, really didn't want to crash into that tooth. For about the fifteenth time, I checked my seat belt.

Our pilot, the bazillionaire computer scientist Ashley Hawking, was rambling about the annoying birds that nested on the island. But I didn't care about finches or swallows. An eagle could have chest-bumped my window and it would not have shifted my focus. If we continued on our current course, we were going to smash into the jagged wall like an egg launched from a slingshot.

The plane's engine roared.

My stomach spun.

Next to me, my brother was staring straight ahead, eyes bulging, with his thin black notebook computer open on his lap. I grabbed his shoulder. His muscles were as solid as rocks and his face was a greenish shade of white. "Matt?" I asked. "Is she pulling up?"

His mouth barely opened. "I hope so," he mumbled.

Our sister, Ava, was sitting in the row behind us, watching the flashing red and green numbers on the electronic control panel. A vein on the side of her head pulsed. She didn't notice me staring back at her. Meanwhile, Ashley Hawking was grinning so wide I could see the edges of her smile from my seat directly behind her. Our mentor, the geek-famous inventor Henry Witherspoon, or Hank, glanced back at me from the co-pilot's seat, his awkward smile flashing too many teeth. Was he trying to make us feel better? If so, he was failing.

Hank leaned over to Ashley. He held his hand out flat and swooped it up toward the roof of the cockpit. "Should we, you know, ascend?"

"What?" Hawking asked. "No! Of course not. Ascend? I thought you knew!"

"Knew what?"

Hawking let go of the controls and waved her hands in a sweeping motion. She sighed with disappointment. "This is one of yours!"

"One of my what?" Hank asked.

"One of your designs!"

Hank spun in his seat, scanning the interior. His mouth was all bunched to one side. He was squinting. And he was completely stumped. Only Hank Witherspoon would struggle to recognize one of his own inventions. His mind was so productive that he dropped out new ideas with about as much thought as a chicken laying eggs.

Matt reached forward with one of his long arms and pointed. "Ummm . . . cliff?"

"What was that?" Hawking yelled back.

We couldn't have been more than a few football fields away from the rock wall. "I think he's wondering if we're planning to avoid that cliff," I said.

Below us, out the left side of the plane and far from the island, a large dock with two boats tied to the sides floated in the middle of the ocean. The water was neon blue and smooth as glass. We probably could've landed on it, but I hadn't noticed any pontoons when we climbed into the aircraft that morning. The thing clearly wasn't a seaplane. So the only safe choices were up, right, or left. And if Ashley Hawking didn't pick one of those soon, we'd keep heading straight. Into the cliffs. We'd be smashed to bits, and all the headlines would read, "Four Geniuses Die as Plane Crashes into Tooth."

No, I wouldn't be the fourth. That honor would belong

to Ashley Hawking. The world would mourn the loss of the two accomplished adults and my brilliant brother and ingenious sister. Me? I might be mentioned in the story somewhere, but I'm no brainiac. I'm average. Maybe a little above, but not by much, and only through effort. I have to work hard, and read all the time, to keep up with the geniuses.

But anyway. Back to that nasty nine-hundred-foot-tall cliff sticking straight up out of the water in front of us. Maybe the *Millennium Falcon* could have made the turn, swooping up at the last second, but I wasn't liking our chances. "Ms. Hawking?"

"Ashley! I told you already. Ashley. And not because I think of you as an equal. Not at all." She laughed to herself. "I simply prefer the sound of my first name. Now, honestly, Hank, someone of your intelligence . . . I assumed you'd see."

Hank was panicking now, his head turning from side to side in jerks, like a broken sprinkler. "I don't . . . when . . ."

Suddenly my sister leaned forward and pointed at a large orange button in the ceiling, covered by a clear plastic case. "Are you serious?" she said with excitement. "Is this the underplane?"

"Yes!" Ashley fake head-butted the dashboard a few times, then looked up to the ceiling. "The child gets the answer. Finally!"

Although Ava was relieved, I found this news to be more than a little frightening. "You made a plane out of underwear?" I asked.

The moment the words escaped I realized I'd probably misunderstood. But no one noticed. Or at least no one bothered to make fun of me. Not yet, anyway. Ava and Matt were pretty skilled at remembering my mistakes, though.

"This is the underplane?" Hank asked. His eyebrows rose so high they nearly touched the top of his head. "You actually built it?"

"I did. But enough talk. You're right, Jack," she said, swiveling around to look me in the eye. "We are getting awfully close, aren't we?" I nodded. The acknowledgment was nice, but I really wanted her to turn back around. "Are we buckled? Good. Would you like to do the honors, Hank?"

"You've tested it?"

"Of course! Once. But it worked beautifully. Go ahead. Press it. Do it. Now."

"You've only tested it once?"

On the dashboard between them, a number in the center of the screen was blinking red and decreasing rapidly. "Yes, once, and a thousand times in simulation. Be confident in your ideas, Hank! Press the button already." She pointed to the flashing red number, which just kept dropping. "Really. Now. Three hundred meters is pushing things. I haven't felt this much adrenaline since I climbed Everest."

Matt mumbled something about the cliff.

Hank hesitated.

Ashley had Manga eyes.

I don't know what Ava was thinking or doing.

But this was no time to sit and wait. I slouched forward in my seat, reached up with my right foot, flicked open the plastic covering, and kicked in the orange button with the heel of my high-top sneaker.

Ashley let out a long, almost disappointed breath. "Finally," she said.

Hank had his right hand out, three fingers extended. He counted down from three. A moment later, the engine stalled. The aircraft turned strangely quiet, as if we were suddenly flying in a giant paper plane.

"Now the chute?" Ava asked.

Before anyone could respond, something exploded behind us.

Yet nobody but me panicked.

Ava put her hand on my shoulder. "A rocket-launched parachute," she explained. "Don't worry. That was supposed to happen."

Firing a parachute out with a rocket didn't make sense to me, but the plane slowed, rattling like an old roller coaster, then began circling to the left. Away from the cliffs. So I exhaled. The lonely floating dock came into view ahead of us. Out through the window, I noticed two wooden boats rounding the corner of the island. Matt was staring at his computer screen again, mumbling to himself. He had a big test coming up, and he'd been studying constantly. One of the downsides of being a genius is that everyone expected you to ace all your tests. I don't think Hank cared, though. Matt put more pressure on himself than anyone else did. But was this really a good time to prepare for an astronomy exam? No. So I reached across and closed his laptop. He didn't protest, which was pretty much a thank-you.

"Wow, it works," Ava said.

"I told you I'd tested it."

"Yeah, once," Ava noted.

"And a thousand times in simulation," Hank added.

The others laughed. Apparently this was funny.

Normally I avoided asking for an explanation when everyone else understood. Hank was always saying there's no such thing as a dumb question, but I was pretty sure I proved him wrong twice a day. And I hated reminding them that I lived on a lower level of the brain game. But there were times I needed to know. "What does 'in simulation' mean?"

Ashley looked back at me like I'd just asked the difference between salt and pepper.

"It's a computerized version of reality, Jack," Hank explained.

"It's like the difference between Street Racer and an actual street race, with real cars," Ava added.

Now I understood. She knew how to speak my language. See, I was actually kind of awesome at Street Racer, and I had this feeling that I'd be a sick driver in the real world, too.

A brown, wide-winged bird swooped in front of us. "Is that a petrel?" Matt asked.

"They're frequent visitors to the island," Ashley said.

Great. Now they were bird-watching, and yet we were still in a plane without pontoons, gliding over the ocean without any clear runway in sight. Sure, we were finally descending, but the underplane turned about as easily as the *Titanic*. As we swung closer to the cliff, I held my breath. No one spoke. I'm not sure anyone even breathed. Ashley and Hank leaned to their left, as if that might help, and the tip of our right wing passed within ten feet of the rocks. Next to me, Matt's face was still that greenish-white color, and he was breathing carefully and gripping the armrests with enough force to dent them.

"That was close!" Ashley said, her voice more excited than relieved.

"So, umm, what's next?" I asked.

"Well, you see, this is the first phase of the transition," Hank said. "The first parachute allows for a more gradual descent, but there's also a braking chute to slow us down further."

"And then?" I pressed.

Hank's eyebrows arched twice. "Wait and see," he said.

Ava tapped me on the shoulder. "Don't worry, I think you're going to like this. It is called 'the underplane,' after all."

I still didn't get what boxers or briefs had to do with the five of us landing safely. But I wasn't about to ask. "So, about that braking chute . . . can we use it now?"

"Not until we slow to thirty miles per hour."

Hank cocked his head to the side, struggling for a view of the parachute suspended above us. "Amazing. Truly. I don't know how to thank you, Ashley. I never thought anyone would ever build one."

The plane soared through a wide loop. We were still about the height of a four-story building from the glassy sea. We swung toward the rock face of Nihoa again, only this time at half the speed and with much less chance of crashing. The color in Matt's face had not changed, but I knew better than to ask him how he was feeling. When Matt was hurt or sick, he didn't want anyone to know. He'd rather hide off by himself somewhere than let you see him aching.

The two boats came into view again. They looked like museum pieces. The masts were tall, the sails all rolled up, and a few people on either side were digging into the water with long black paddles. "What are those?" I asked.

Ashley Hawking squinted, gagged for a three-count, then breathed in, shook her head, and smiled. "Friends of mine," she said. "They think we're enemies, but as I'm sure you know, kids, those two are one and the same. As Sun Tzu said, you should treat your enemies as if they are your best friends."

"Is he one of those jazz guys, Hank?" I asked. Our mentor had strange taste in music, but I was growing to like some of the tunes. I'd been trying to learn their names to impress him.

"No, that's Sun Ra, and he only really began as a jazz pianist—"

Another jolt cut his answer short. Ava pointed to the control panel. Our speed was dropping rapidly. And we were circling closer and closer to the water. Hank turned. I thought he was checking to see if we were okay, but he stared out the small rearview window instead. His smile vanished. "You used a larger braking chute."

"Yes," Ashley said. "I had to. In simulation, the chute you suggested didn't slow the plane quickly enough. Your design was completely inadequate. No offense."

Hank paused before answering. "None taken?"

We were at least a few city blocks away from the island, gliding through our third full circle, cruising at the speed of a bike down a steep hill, when the plane finally skimmed the surface of the sea.

We bounced.

Hank whooped.

Ashley hollered.

Then we bounced again and again, lower each time, like a stone skipping across the water.

Ava quietly beamed, and my still-green brother relaxed his grip. When we finally stopped, my heart was thumping. My hands were cramped. Apparently, Matt wasn't the only one squeezing the armrests. I looked out the window. We had to be a mile away from the shore. Was this really the right place to land? Were we floating? Or sinking? And what did all this have to do with underwear?

Ecstatic, Hank pointed to the button on the roof, then asked Ashley, "May I?"

"You're the guest," Ashley said.

Hank pushed the button with the heel of his hand. Above me, something clicked. A thud followed, somewhere behind us. Then two loud hisses on either side of the plane. Below me, I heard the sound of rushing water, like a quickly filling toilet bowl. Suddenly I needed to go to the bathroom, but there were more important things happening.

Glancing out the window, I noticed that the wings were dropping below the surface. The plane was sinking. And no one else onboard seemed particularly bothered. "This is supposed to happen?" I asked.

Matt pointed his thumb out the window and swallowed. "Why not shed the wings?" he asked, struggling to get the words out.

"The aerodynamic profile of the wings is hydrodynami-cally efficient, too," Hank answered. "In both cases, you're just moving through a fluid."

Ava put her hand on my shoulder. She wore several colorful beaded rings. "What he means," she began, leaning forward, "is that you don't need to drop the wings because—"

"I know," I said. And I didn't, really, but the geniuses are always explaining things to me, and I wasn't in the mood for a lesson. So I pulled out my new notebook. Before we'd left for Hawaii I had a great idea. Or a great idea for me, anyway. Whenever the geniuses said something I didn't understand, I'd jot down a little note about it, then do some research later and learn about it on my own. That way I wouldn't have to admit it when I wasn't following along. And sure, I could've checked on my phone, but then they'd notice. I held the notebook down in the space between my left leg

and the side of the plane, so Matt couldn't see, and scribbled "hydrodynamic" on a blank page. After a second, I added "Sun Something"—unfortunately, I'd already forgotten the name of the guy Ashley quoted.

The plane was sinking faster. The dock with the two boats was only a few pool lengths away; part of me wished we could've just swum over. But the blue water was already climbing up the sides. The surface reached the bottom of my window, then rose higher and higher until it climbed over the top. A few seconds later, the underplane dropped below the surface and began gliding down through the blue sea.

Oh.

Right.

The *underplane*. As in *underwater plane*. Not an aircraft made out of old boxer shorts.

Our ride had transformed into a six-seat submarine.

Since we met Hank seven months ago, I'd been introduced to all kinds of strange machines and vehicles and experiences. I'd been to the bottom of the world and fought off a crazy Australian and flown in an inflatable vehicle that wasn't supposed to fly. I'd even had some experiences with miniature subs, since my sister had built one. But I'd never been inside an actual submarine. And certainly not in the Pacific Ocean, with who knows how much water or how many deadly creatures lurking below me. On the one-to-ten scale of soul-stretching, brain-twisting experiences, I'd give this one a fourteen.

The water was filled with specks that sparkled in the sunlight. A group of long silver fish darted past our windows. I'd always imagined that riding in a submarine would be like staring at the fish tanks in an aquarium. But now it felt as if we were the ones trapped in the tank. And I kind of wanted to get back to the air. "So that was fun," I said, "but can we go back up now?"

My ears popped.

"Up? Of course not," Ashley said.

The underplane nosed down in the direction of the island. But we weren't going to Nihoa. Not yet. Far below us, an enormous, brightly lit underwater building hung below the dock. It looked like the headquarters of some kind of powerful secret society or nefarious villain. The outside was swarming with huge fish.

"You still want to go back up, Jack?" Ava asked.

I could practically hear her smiling. "No," I said with a grin. "Not anymore."